CROWE'S FEAT

SOMETIMES THE "EVERYMAN" IS THE ONLY MAN FOR THE JOB

E.W. NICKERSON

Order this book online at www.trafford.com
or email orders@trafford.com

Most Trafford titles are also available at major online book retailers.

Author photo by Betty McDowell.

Printed in the United States of America.

ISBN: 978-1-4669-1515-2 (sc)
ISBN: 978-1-4669-1516-9 (hc)
ISBN: 978-1-4669-1514-5 (e)

Library of Congress Control Number: 2012902715

Trafford rev. 03/28/2012

 www.trafford.com

North America & international
toll-free: 1 888 232 4444 (USA & Canada)
phone: 250 383 6864 ♦ fax: 812 355 4082

Author's Note

This novel is fiction but based, in part, on an actual event.

On April 17th 1984 there were shots fired from the then Libyan Embassy in St. James Sq., London. Ten people were hurt, and Women Police Constable, Yvonne Fletcher was killed. She was 25 years of age.

On February 1st 1985 a memorial was unveiled by Prime Minister Margaret Thatcher.

A photo of the Memorial is shown on the back cover.

Out of respect for WPC Fletcher and her family, her name is not used in the novel.

Ed Nickerson

I would like to thank my wife Judy and my friends Sue Manson and Gordon Nash for their help, assistance, and direction in helping me on this my second novel.

CHAPTER ONE

SATURDAY, SEPTEMBER 29TH 1984

• • ● ● ● ● • •

"You make a mean breakfast, Ed," Carolyn said, sipping her tea. She smiled up at him as he gathered the dishes for the dishwasher.

"I must have got my enthusiasm for a great meal from our discussions last night," he replied, closing the dishwasher and pressing the buttons.

"We barely spoke as I recall," she said, raising her eyebrows.

He thought for a moment. "I seem to recall you saying some very complimentary things. Let me think . . ."

"Don't embarrass me please," Carolyn said, interrupting him and closing her eyes.

"I would never do that, Carolyn," he said, sitting down at the table and taking her hand in his. "Just keep in mind that I love you and last night was a wonderful experience for me. Best birthday I've ever had." He kissed her hand. "More tea?"

"Please, and thank you. Last night was wonderful," she agreed, "and while I do not say it as often as you do, Ed, I do love you. Please always know that."

Ed stood up to pour them more tea.

They had left The Queen's Head the night before, Carolyn having surprised him with an unannounced visit. There was business to talk about, but they had agreed it would wait until after breakfast the next morning. The walk from the pub to Ed's apartment had been slow and they had held hands. The conversation was limited to what had happened in each other's lives since they had last seen each other in England five months earlier.

Within moments of entering the apartment they were in each other's arms, holding, touching, and kissing as if their worlds were coming to an end. Slowly, ever so slowly, they had undressed and made their way to Ed's bed. They had carefully and tenderly touched and caressed each other throughout, and shared in climaxing their love at the same time.

When they awoke at seven, with the sunshine breaking through the window, they made love once more.

"Nice flat," Carolyn said, looking around. "Too bad you didn't turn the lights on for me to see it last night."

"You seemed to have other things on your mind," Ed said, putting her cup of tea in front of her. "And it's an apartment, remember?"

"Just testing you," she laughed.

"Oh, I'm really quite Canadian now, Miss Andrews. I even drive my car to go shopping three blocks from here!"

"And do you buy frozen food, with enough in your freezer to last three months?"

"Absolutely," Ed said. "It's the Canadian way. When in Rome and all . . ."

"It looks like you've gained some weight. Half a stone? And your hair is longer. Is this the new you?"

Ed sucked his in waist. "Five pounds. Not enough activity in the love-making area perhaps?" He combed his hand through his jet black hair that was certainly longer than usual. "When I return," he said, more to himself than Carolyn.

They carried their tea to the balcony and sat. The view overlooked Sixteen Mile Creek in downtown Oakville. Several yachts were moving out onto Lake Ontario, using their motors to enter into the lake. The muffled sounds were comforting as they watched the yachts glide through. On each vessel crewmembers were ready to drop the sails as they entered the lake.

"Beautiful." Carolyn said. "I could easily become jealous."

"It is lovely," Ed agreed, putting his hand on her head and gently pulling her to his side. "Why don't you move in?"

Carolyn smiled, closing her eyes and nodding gently as she did. They both knew that was never going to happen, but they also understood that Ed's question was more of a statement of his fondness.

"How's your mother?" Ed asked, changing the subject.

2

"My mother is still my mother, Ed. But she does ask after you from time to time."

"Happy that I'm in Canada is she? Away from her daughter and all."

"Actually I think she rather likes you. She's got over the fact that I'm not going to marry her best friend's son, and truth be told I think she is silently pleased about that. Bearing in mind," Carolyn added, "that 'silently' is not a word that comes to the fore when thinking of my mother's opinions."

"I always thought she had good taste," Ed added, nodding his head in approval.

Carolyn smiled. "Can we go inside and talk business?"

"Of course we can," Ed said, standing and sliding open the screen door to the apartment, "and I promise to try and keep my hands off you as we talk."

They entered the apartment and sat on separate chesterfields facing each other.

"So is it hostages in Libya you really wanted to talk about?" Ed asked, leaning back into the chesterfield.

"Isn't that what I mentioned last night?" Carolyn replied, feigning amazement in her look.

"It was indeed," Ed agreed. "But then I'm getting a little used to having people such as yourself speak carefully in public, and The Queen's Head is public . . . in more ways than one I might add."

Carolyn nodded her understanding. "Very clever," she laughed.

"Well?" Ed prompted.

Carolyn shook her head gently. "No, it is not the *hostages* in Libya I came here to talk about."

He leaned forward and spread his hands. "Well? Should I bring my English-Arabic translation book?"

"Do you have one?"

"No."

She winked at him. "Too bad. You'll have to wait until we get to England I'm afraid. In this case I'm just the messenger, and the message is that, 'C', my father that is, would like to talk to you. Please don't ask me more. I don't want to have to lie to you."

Ed nodded. "I understand Carolyn. I am more than happy that you're the messenger. What's the time frame? I have things to . . ."

Carolyn interrupted. "We leave in two hours, Ed."

"What? I er . . ," Ed mumbled.

"It's all arranged. Pat Weston from Ottawa will look after your arrangements here including your work, mail, phone messages, etc. I'm sorry to dump this on you like this, but you'll recall we agreed last night not to talk about the details until today." She winked as she reminded him of the agreement.

"You've got me there," he agreed. "But how do you know I don't have a date for tonight? It is Saturday after all."

"Pat Weston said you don't have any such plans, and I had no reason to suppose otherwise." She cringed as she spoke.

"What a loser I am," he chuckled, and walked to his bedroom to pack. "Loser, loser, loser," he muttered.

Carolyn said nothing, but lifted the phone and started dialing.

Ed walked out from his bedroom with his bag packed, ready to go. "So is this what you English call a Command Performance?" he asked, with a wide smile.

"No," Carolyn replied smugly, "it's what you Canadians call a trip to the old country to see if we still eat cold toast and drink warm beer."

"And do you?"

"Absolutely!" Carolyn said in a posh voice. "We don't change. We are British after all."

"Yeah, right," Ed said chuckling. "Mrs. Thatcher might not agree with you about changing."

"Got your passport?" Carolyn asked.

"Got it."

"The answer to your question, in all seriousness, Ed, is—no, you don't have to accept this assignment. If you decline now, that is not an issue. We make love one more time," she said, nodding toward his bedroom, "and I fly back home alone."

"Hmm," he said, rubbing his chin in thought, "that sounds like a good alternative."

She smiled up at him. "Is that your choice then?"

"No, I don't think so," he said, looking around. "I need a change of scenery, and who better to see that with than a rich, older English lady."

"And one that you love."

He nodded several times. "That too, I suppose."

"Good, then let's get going," Carolyn said, standing and picking up her small travel bag. She turned to face him. "By the way, Ed, do you know you told me that you loved me seventeen times last night?"

He grinned broadly. "No, I wasn't counting. At least not that. What I counted only got to three."

She gently shook her head and winked. "Maybe that's the difference between men and women?"

"Or the difference between the English and Canadians?" he offered.

"We'll have to come to some agreement on that" Carolyn laughed.

"Good choice of words," he added, kissing her forehead. He pulled her close to him and held her slim body to his own. "Five foot two and eyes of blue," he whispered.

"I'm five foot four," she said, looking up at him.

"Five foot four, with eyes I adore."

"Let's get out of here," she decided, walking to the door, "before we change your mind!"

The limousine was waiting for them in the entranceway to his apartment building. Ed recognized the driver and the second man in the front of the vehicle. They were Sergeants Tyson and McDowell who had driven the limousine during Ed's initial involvement with MI6 during Operation Niagara five months earlier. They did not get out of the vehicle, but raised their hands to Ed and Carolyn in recognition. Ed and Carolyn faced each other in the rear of the limousine, and it pulled gently into the traffic.

"May I ask you a personal question?" Ed asked. "Personal for me, that is."

Carolyn nodded.

"How does Pat Weston know so much about me? I haven't seen her since I arrived back in Canada; except for last night, of course."

"To be blunt, Ed, it's part of her job. To ensure your safety, that is. We still have to assume that the PKK are still active in the Toronto area."

He thought about that for a while. He had been kidnapped and then negotiated the freedom of hostages with the PKK, a Kurdish separatist party in Turkey, during his first involvement with MI6. That all seemed a long time ago, but was only five months earlier. "She hasn't got a hidden microphone in my apartment or anything like that has she?"

Carolyn shook her head. "Nothing like that. Not even close. That would be breaking all of the rules. Keep in mind she's on our side."

"Well if she did, last night would have been interesting listening," Ed smiled.

"Not your standard Friday night activity, Mr. Crowe?"

Ed looked at her sideways.

Carolyn gagged in response. "Sorry, I shouldn't have asked that even in humor. Please, please accept my apology. That was totally rude of me." She leaned over and touched his hands.

"Apology accepted, and indiscreet compliment taken," he said. "But, oh so not the case."

She raised a hand. "Let's drop the point, and please forget I could be so rude."

"I have phoned Pat several times since I came to Canada," Ed offered.

"Yes, I know. Seven times."

"I left messages. She never responded, not once."

"I know that too."

"I just wanted to make sure you knew."

Carolyn nodded. "Thanks."

"So where are we going?" Ed wondered, looking out of the window.

"Hamilton airport."

Ed knew that the airport in Hamilton had been enlarged recently and it was considerably closer than either of the two Toronto airports.

"We'll likely be the only plane flying out today." Carolyn spoke flatly, still uneasy about her remark. She felt she had broken a bond between them, and it hurt.

"I thought we'd agreed to forget your comment," Ed said seriously.

She shook her head, keeping her eyes down. "I just feel so stupid, as though I've created a rift between us." She looked up at him, trying to smile.

"I recall the movie said something about love meaning not having to say sorry?"

"That's true," she agreed, "but I'm still sorry."

"And for the nineteenth time, I love you. So please, please forget it. My only regret is that I couldn't think of anything quickly enough to respond to your question." He leaned over to her and kissed her forehead. "Your punishment is that the next time I see your mother I'm going to tell her what you asked me, having to explain the full details of the previous night's activities of course."

She smiled, pushing him away. "You wouldn't! I'd never speak to you again."

"You mention the issue again and I will. You put it behind you, and I'll never mention it."

"Which issue is that?" she asked innocently.

"My point exactly," he said, closing the discussion forever.

Ed went back to looking out of the window to get his bearings. Carolyn sat back in the seat and let the guilt flow from her mind, gone now forever. She felt closer to Ed than she had ever felt for anyone. She smiled inwardly; comfortable in their relationship, but knowing it could never be what she wanted it to be.

Ed turned to Carolyn, now curious as to Pat's knowledge of his activities. "So tell me, does Pat know what I had for supper on Thursday?"

Carolyn shook her head. "No . . . . But on Tuesday you had pizza and a couple of glasses of wine." She could not hide her grin.

"Whoa!" Ed exclaimed. "That's scary. How could she . . . you?"

"And you ate alone."

"Hey now! How do you know that, and how do you know I didn't have a young lady join me?"

"Credit cards, young man, credit cards. Pat can see whatever you buy using them. Remember she set them up for you initially."

Ed shook his head. "And the young lady?"

"You ordered a medium pizza after picking up a bottle of wine. Half the pizza is in your freezer section of your fridge, correctly wrapped I might add, and the bottle of wine is in your cupboard, half finished— thus you ate alone. Elementary, my dear Watson."

"You looked into my fridge?"

She nodded, feigning an apologetic grin. "That was personal. Besides, I knew that without looking."

Ed was now seriously curious. "Okay, the rest makes sense, but how else would you know I was alone?"

Carolyn leaned forward to whisper. "Well the way you went at me last night . . ."

"Oh, my God," Ed groaned, rolling his eyes, "oh, my bloody God."

"Absence makes the . . ."

"Stop right there, Miss Andrews. Just stop right there." He took her hands in his and kissed them. "Not only are you beautiful and intelligent and a wonderful friend, you're also the sneakiest person I've ever met!"

"Why thank you," Carolyn answered proudly. "What a nice thing for you to say."

Hamilton airport was under re-construction. Originally constructed in 1940, it was built to support the British Commonwealth Air Force training program for the Second World War. The current renovations were to expand the growing need for air travel in the southern Ontario area.

The limousine drove around the construction and onto the runway. The plane, a small jet, was at one end of the runway with its door open and the stairway in place.

They quickly got on board. The pilot and co-pilot packed their bags, quickly went over the rules and within five minutes the plane was in the air, heading east.

The five-hour flight was relaxing. Carolyn updated Ed on her role in Bulgaria, touching on the many changes in the surrounding countries. The historic changes taking place in the USSR were affecting all of Eastern Europe in many different ways.

Ed related that Mr. Cooper, the General, had sold his travel agency and was now retired. Carolyn was surprised to learn that the General was closing in on seventy.

"He looks so much younger," Carolyn said, thinking back to her meeting him just five months ago.

"Maybe working with . . ." Ed paused, and finished his sentence in a whisper, "MI6, keeps you young?"

Carolyn whispered back. "I hope so. Maybe we'll grow young together?"

"That would be nice," Ed replied, keeping his voice low, "but I'm only a lowly consultant. And remember a consultant only tells you what you already know, but were afraid to admit!"

Carolyn waved him off. "You may be a consultant but certainly not lowly, at least in the mind of my father. And," she continued, pointing a finger at him, "my father has a very good mind."

"Yes, ma'am." Ed said in agreement, saluting as he spoke. He gave her a quick smile and walked to the back of the plane. "Tea or coffee for madam?"

The plane landed in the same airfield that had been used previously when flying Ed on MI6 'business', and the same car with the same driver picked them up. Ed and Carolyn slid in the back seat and the car pulled away, heading into the countryside. The weather was cloudy with a gentle rain. The local time was gone 9 p.m., and it looked as if the rain was going to stay.

"May I ask?" Ed said, looking at Carolyn.

"Of course," she grinned. "We're heading straight to Stonebridge Manor to see my father."

"Will Mr. Cooper, or should I say the General, be there?"

"Yes. As your joint sponsor, my being the other of course, we'll both be in attendance."

"Protecting my rear end, so to speak?"

"I'd never thought of it that way," she laughed. "More to ensure you're the right person for the challenge ahead is the way I look at it."

"So tell me, Carolyn," he asked, looking at her eye to eye, "do you know what the challenge, as you put it, is?"

Carolyn thought for a second. "I would have to say yes," she paused, "and no!"

"Is that a formal wait-and-see and stop asking so many questions, or—I know some things, but not all of the details, and stop asking so many questions?"

She nodded once. "That would be a yes!"

"Well we're almost there," he muttered. "I might as well wait until I speak with the boss. I'm not getting anything out of you, am I?"

She nodded. "That would be a yes," she paused, "and a no."

"To change the subject to one less secretive," he said dryly, "is your mother at the Manor, and will I see her?"

"Alas, yes she is. No, she does not know you're arriving as a guest, and I have no doubt she will want to say hello and find out as much about you as she can."

"Ah, I see."

"This is the main reason, if you will excuse our bad manners, that you will be driven to the Inn tonight and not join us as a guest until the morning."

"I understand fully," he said. "And tomorrow I will be going where?"

She waved off the question. "Here we are, Mr. Crowe, Stonebridge Manor."

He picked up on the message. "Thank you for picking me up and delivering me safely, Miss Andrews. You are a charming and delightful messenger."

She winked at him. "What a nice thing to say, Mr. Crowe, but be sure to save some of your charm for Lady Stonebridge."

Ed was always amazed by Stonebridge Manor. A three minute drive from the automated gate and unseen for half the drive, it stood in splendor in the English countryside, with the private forest set behind it to make it a perfect setting for the longtime Stonebridge family home.

Lady Stonebridge opened the door as they walked up the steps. As was usual, she was dressed so as not to be caught off-guard if the Queen drove up unexpectedly. She opened the door fully, allowing them to get in from the rain. After they had entered she closed the door and turned to them.

"What a lovely surprise, Mr. Crowe," she said quietly, "and my world-traveling daughter with you. Why this is absolutely wonderful." She took his arm and steered him to the family room.

Carolyn followed one step behind. "Good evening, Mother."

"Good evening, dear." She replied without turning. "Do order some tea, dear. I'm sure Mr. Crowe must want a cup of tea. Isn't that correct, Mr. Crowe?"

Ed sat on the chair Lady Stonebridge had walked him to. "That would be lovely, Lady Stonebridge."

Carolyn raised her eyes and rang the small bell from the table. Immediately the maid entered the room. Carolyn ordered tea and biscuits.

Lady Stonebridge took her seat, keeping a straight back as she perched on the edge. Her short and slim stature was far from her sharp and inquisitive nature. "Mr. Crowe, how are you? It is still Mr. Crowe isn't it? I do understand that some of my husband's associates do use different names from time to time."

Before he could respond, Carolyn replied. "Of course it's still Mr. Crowe, Mother. And don't forget we have an appointment upstairs."

"Why thank you, dear," Lady Stonebridge replied without taking her eyes off Ed. "And I don't doubt Mr. Crowe can respond quite capably to my questions. Isn't that correct, Mr. Crowe?"

"That would be a yes, Lady Stonebridge," he replied, bowing his head ever so gently. Carolyn smiled from behind Lady Stonebridge.

"Good, good," Lady Stonebridge continued. "Now do tell me all about Canada."

Ed briefly explained his new job, where he lived, his visitors from England, and the differences and the similarities between England and Canada. He finished just as the tea was delivered.

"That sounds wonderful, Mr. Crowe," Lady Stonebridge said, taking a sip of tea. "Now Oakville, is that anywhere near Ottawa? That's where you lived for a while wasn't it, dear?" She turned to Carolyn.

"No, Mother," she answered. "The cities are about two hundred and fifty miles apart. Would you agree, Mr. Crowe?"

Ed nodded his head. "I would say about that, although I've never visited there. I do have a friend there, however, so I will likely visit there soon."

"I see," Lady Stonebridge said, wanting to get control of the conversation. "And is your friend also in the travel business?"

Ed saw the smile on Carolyn's face.

"No she works for the federal government." Ed smiled gently as he spoke, and took a sip of tea.

"Well that is nice," Lady Stonebridge said, wanting to turn to see Carolyn's reaction. But she kept her eyes on Ed.

"Oakville sounds like such a nice place to live," Lady Stonebridge continued. "Have you ever been there, dear?" She turned to Carolyn as she spoke.

"Just to pick up Mr. Crowe, Mother. Just there and back again."

"I see," Lady Stonebridge said slowly. "You should be more careful with your words my dear. I'm sure you meant to say—to collect Mr. Crowe. There can be such a difference of interpretation in today's world."

"Point taken, Mother."

Ed continued the process of drinking his tea, although he had emptied the cup some time earlier.

"One more question, Mr. Crowe?" Lady Stonebridge put her cup down.

"Of course, Lady Stonebridge," Ed replied. Carolyn had closed her eyes and was hoping for the best.

"How is your mother? I'm sure she misses you, as any mother would when their child is so far away."

Carolyn had a mild look of guilt. Ed thought about the question.

"Being rather close as we are," Ed said, "I think it is fair to say that we do miss each other. Luckily phone calls are rather cheap, and she has visited me once."

"That is a very thoughtful response, very thoughtful indeed." She stood and motioned to the door.

"May I ask a question of you, Lady Stonebridge?" Ed asked. Carolyn silently gasped, eyes wide open.

"Of course, Mr. Crowe," Lady Stonebridge replied. "How may I be of assistance?"

"I was wondering if I could take the biscuits with us. I have not eaten since your very organized daughter *collected* me from my apartment this morning."

Carolyn quickly picked up the plate of biscuits, cringing in guilt as she did.

"Please take them, Mr. Crowe," Lady Stonebridge smiled. "I will arrange for sandwiches to be sent up to the office."

Ed nodded his thanks.

"Have a good meeting, Mr. Crowe. I trust this event does not result in a further black eye." She was referring to the events of Operation Niagara when she and Ed had met for the first time.

Ed and Carolyn left the room and headed up the stairs to her father's office.

When Ed and Carolyn entered Lord Stonebridge's office both he and Mr. Cooper were by the window commenting on the rain and the end of summer. They quickly turned and welcomed them. Lord Stonebridge was tall, at least two inches above Ed's six foot. He was athletically built, from what Ed had assumed was a military background. Mr. Cooper, the 'General' in the MI6 circle, was visibly healthier and more relaxed since Ed had seen him last. After everyone shook hands and exchanged greetings, Lord Stonebridge motioned for all to take a seat. He sat at his desk and looked around at each of them, smiling as he did so.

"Well, well," he said, "to use an overused welcome, it's been a long time."

"Lots of changes since we last met in this room." Mr. Cooper commented.

"Indeed, that is so," Lord Stonebridge nodded. "The General has retired, from his full-time job at least. Miss Andrews is now in Bulgaria. And Mr. Crowe has started a new life in Canada."

They all nodded in agreement.

"And I am still in the same old job as I was five months ago." He pulled a face. "Perhaps I need a change also?"

"Job too boring for you is it then?" Mr. Cooper asked in humor.

"Never boring, General, never boring." He stood up, walked to the window, looked out for a few moments, and then turned to face them. "Which brings us to today's situation." He sat back at his desk.

"First I want to thank you all for joining me today. Secondly I should, indeed I must, remind you that we are bound to keep today's discussion secret. And finally let me say that I have ordered tea. As soon as it arrives we will proceed."

As if by magic there was a knock on the door and the maid entered with a tray of tea. Several sandwiches were also included. After the sandwiches were eaten and tea poured, they each took their respective seats.

"How good is your memory, Mr. Crowe?" Lord Stonebridge asked, leaning back in his seat. He didn't wait for an answer. "Do you recall the events of April 17th of this year?"

Ed looked up, thinking if the date meant anything to him.

"Nothing jumps to mind, sir" Ed said. "Except, of course, I was personally in the process of planning my trip to Turkey."

Lord Stonebridge continued. "What if I mention the Libyan Embassy in London?"

Ed immediately recalled the event. It had shaken London and Londoners to the core.

"That would be the day people were shot at from the Libyan Embassy, and a female Police Officer died. Others were also shot and injured, although I do not recall how many."

Lord Stonebridge nodded. "Ten other people were hurt."

"A very sad day for international relations," Mr. Cooper added.

"Ten days later," Lord Stonebridge continued, "the staff of the embassy simply walked out of the building and went home to Libya. No one was ever charged with the shootings or the murder."

Carolyn took the time, during a lull in the conversation, to top-up everyone's tea. She smiled quickly as she filled Ed's cup.

"And today?" she asked as she took her seat.

"Yes today," Lord Stonebridge repeated quietly. "Today," he said, now speaking louder and faster, "we are going to discuss the possibility of bringing the killer to justice. That is to bring him back to London, not as a protected member of a foreign embassy, but as the cold blooded killer which indeed he is."

"Well that sounds easy," Ed said. "We just fly in, grab the man, and fly home."

Carolyn gave Ed a look. She turned to Lord Stonebridge. "What do we know, sir? You mentioned it was a 'him'. Do we know for sure who we are after? If so, do we know where he is? I assume he's in Libya?"

"Mr. Crowe may be closer than you may think," Lord Stonebridge said. "But to answer your questions first. We are sure who the killer is. It is indeed a man. He was a guard at the embassy. And yes, he lives in Libya."

Mr. Cooper took over. "And while we might have considered one shot an accident or a terrible mistake, so many shots and so many injured is totally unacceptable." He rubbed his chin. "The price has to be paid."

"That, incidentally, is a direct quote from my superior," Lord Stonebridge emphasized. "The price has to be paid."

"Surely this isn't entirely political?" Carolyn asked.

"No, Miss Andrews," Mr. Cooper said. "Her remarks were in response to our recommendations. Her initial thoughts were: how should I say this? Somewhat more dramatic than our recommendations."

"And far more dangerous for them than for us." Lord Stonebridge said. "Suffice to say if we proceeded with her idea we would be planning for a much larger and a heavier armed force than what we want to talk about today."

"But today we're just talking about a young, inexperienced, part-time member of our department?" Carolyn asked, looking seriously at Ed.

"You do have a way with words, I must say," Lord Stonebridge continued. "Perhaps I should fill you in on more of the details, and then we can all sleep on it and meet again in the morning. It is getting late."

Ed was wide-awake, but it was eleven thirty local time.

They all nodded in agreement.

"In summary," Lord Stonebridge said, "there are several positive things to consider." He sat up in his seat. "The relations between the U.K and Libya have been a disaster since the killing. Officially we have not spoken but in fact of course, we have."

"Through an intermediary?" Carolyn asked.

Lord Stonebridge raised his eyebrows. "Indeed," he replied, "through our good friends in Ottawa. Many good relations were built between Ottawa and ourselves as a result of Operation Niagara, and it is safe to say their new prime minister, Brian Mulroney, is very much on-side with any help they can offer."

"I smell a Pat." Carolyn murmured, almost to herself.

"Sorry?" Lord Stonebridge asked.

Carolyn adjusted herself in her seat. "I was just wondering if the good relations have been aided by Pat Weston, sir. You may recall she was involved in Operation Niagara?"

"Yes, yes indeed," Stonebridge recalled. "She was Miss Wilson then, and 'officially' died in the operation . . . as Miss Wilson, I mean."

"Yes, sir," Ed added. "She is Miss Weston now, and lives in Ottawa."

Lord Stonebridge continued. "The message to Libya has been clear. We want the man who fired the shots returned to England for prosecution. If that is not arranged, then significant economic sanctions will be put in place. Their oil exportation will be reduced or eliminated, and all imports by sea will be ceased."

"That," Mr. Cooper added, "would result in a crisis not even Colonel Gaddafi could withstand."

"So their official response to our request for the man to be returned to England has been—No. If you want him, come and get him," Lord Stonebridge said. "And by saying that, they mean it. They are willing to give the man up. This is from the highest level."

"So we go in, pick him up, and bring him home," Ed said. "Sounds easy to me."

"Shake your head, Mr. Crowe." Carolyn interrupted. "There must be more to it than that."

"I'm afraid there is." Lord Stonebridge said, smiling. "At the highest level, the message is quite clear. But even in a nation run by one man with the support of the army, politics plays a role. To many in the army, especially among the mid-level and lower-level ranks, our culprit is a hero. So when we go in, or should I say if we go in, we are taking a large risk both politically and personally for those involved."

Lord Stonebridge stood up and stretched his arms. "So that is where we are at. Let's meet again here tomorrow morning at eight, and see what our collective minds can produce."

They left the office in a somber and thoughtful manner.

Carolyn walked Ed to the front entrance of the manor. The limo was running and ready to go.

"The General is staying here tonight, Ed." She said. "I think he and my father want to share a sherry and talk about old times."

"Could I ask you a favor?" Ed asked, winking.

"I don't know, Mr. Crowe," she chuckled, "you do have a way with women."

He tilted his head to the car. "Could you join me for breakfast tomorrow at seven at the Inn? Strictly breakfast."

"That is a lovely idea, Mr. Crowe." She reached over and gently kissed his cheek. "Tomorrow at seven it is."

Ed got into the limo, waved as it pulled away, and felt excited about the possibilities for tomorrow.

CHAPTER TWO

SUNDAY, SEPTEMBER 30TH

• • • ● ● ● ● • •

Ed was sitting on the patio drinking coffee when Carolyn arrived. The rain had cleared overnight and the air was now crisp and clean. The sun was slowly creeping onto the sky, warming everything it touched. Ed stood as she joined him at the table. They sat across from each other.

"Good morning, Ed. You look rather refreshed and in top form."

"Good morning, Carolyn," he replied, bowing gently to her remarks. "I do in fact feel wonderful, thank you. And you look even more beautiful this morning than you did yesterday."

"Sleep helps," she said, smiling and pouring herself coffee.

"Yes, nothing like a good night's sleep is there?"

"I don't think I meant quite that." She kept her eyes on the one page menu. The menu hadn't changed in all of the years she had visited the Inn, but she read it in full, and then looked up.

"Have you ordered?"

"By special request: Canadian bacon, half-inch thick pancakes, maple syrup, and a beer!"

She pulled a face. "I'll have a couple of slices of toast. Cold."

"I'm with you."

The waiter, who was also the manager of the Inn, took their order. Ed recalled that Carolyn had mentioned that the manager carried a gun at all times. Ed looked to see if he could see a bulge in the manager's clothing, but could not.

"It's probably strapped to his ankle," Carolyn said, noticing Ed's not-so-subtle peeking.

"Have you ever fired a gun?" Ed asked, the question almost in a whisper.

She looked up into the sky, thinking. "Would you think better of me if I said yes or no?"

He shrugged. "No difference, just wondering."

"Then yes."

"Wow," he said excitedly, "what's it like? Are you a good shot? Do you have any badges to show you're a marksman? What kind of gun did you use?"

She shook her head. "It's noisy. It hurt my arm, and I got all kinds of crap over my hands. It wasn't any fun."

"Oh, I see." His enthusiasm died.

She smiled and leaned forward. "It was a Smith and Wesson 9 millimeter something-or-other."

"Ah, I see."

"You do?"

He grinned. "No, I have no idea. Saw too many re-runs of Gunsmoke I suppose. That is when my mum would let me watch them. She preferred I watch Dixon of Dock Green."

Carolyn grinned. "At least there is some reality in that. People being shot and not bleeding and every female a dancing girl didn't do it for me."

They shared a laugh as the food arrived.

"So did you come up with any ideas for this mornings meeting?" Ed asked, nibbling on his very cold and very thin toast.

"Nothing positive."

"Anything negative?"

"No."

"Not very excited about it all then?"

She wavered on her response. "I think it's fair to say that I'd be more excited if it was me that might be popping over to Libya. It's not that I'm jealous, but my reason for being at the meeting today is to challenge things, accept nothing, and think of the worse case." She shrugged. "It's my job, that's all. And incidentally, my father fully accepts this as my role. In fact it's his protocols that I'm following."

Ed nodded his understanding.

"Those protocols," she continued, "is why he calls me Miss Andrews. It's his way of separating our roles."

"And why you call him sir?"

"Exactly."

"And of course your real name isn't Miss Andrews?"

"Not my real name, no."

"You'll always be Miss Andrews to me," he said, raising his coffee cup to toast her.

"That's nice, Ed. I appreciate that. I always want to be Miss Andrews to you."

"Even when you're old and gray and married?" he asked.

"Even when I'm old and gray."

They went back to their toast and coffee.

Carolyn looked up at Ed. "So did you come up with any ideas?"

He nodded. "Actually I did."

She looked at him, as he drank his coffee. "So, are you going to fill me in, or wait until we get to the office? As your sponsor I should be entitled to a little respect when it comes to these things," she said, pouting just a bit.

He sat up straight in his chair. "As a sponsor, as a friend, as my favourite Oxford graduate, I'll be happy to expand on my initial considerations. Indeed . . ."

She interrupted. "Just get on with it, Ed. We don't have all day."

He waved her off. "Indeed," he continued, "as my most gracious lover . . ."

"Okay," she said, smiling, "I apologize. But, Ed, get to the point."

He took a final sip of his coffee. "My thinking was, and I confess I have no idea if this will work, would be to again use my Canadian passport, especially—and this is a stroke of luck—since the people in Ottawa are the contact between the British and Libyan government. I could be an addition to the communication process in some fashion. What do you think?"

She looked at him straight on, thinking first, and then smiling.

"What?" he asked. "Is the idea so stupid?"

She closed her eyes and chewed on her bottom lip.

"Well?" he asked.

"I'm trying to think how to respond to your idea."

"Why don't you just come straight to the point? If it doesn't make any sense, I don't want to look like an idiot."

"I think it's an excellent idea. Indeed something my father would think of." She smiled, knowingly.

Ed thought for a moment and then rolled his eyes. "Oh, of course," he laughed. "So excellent in fact to be bloody obvious."

"Let's not say obvious, Ed, let's say strategically and tactically a superior and high-level prime consideration."

Ed nodded slowly. "Very clever, Miss Andrews," he said, standing to leave. "Let's say that shall we. You do have a way with words."

"Moi?" She said, pointing to herself. "Au contraire!"

They walked to the limo, got in, and the car pulled away slowly.

Lord Stonebridge, Mr. Cooper, Carolyn, and Ed were seated in Lord Stonebridge's office at eight sharp. They chatted freely amongst themselves, waiting for the obligatory tea to be delivered.

"So tell me, Mr. Crowe," Lord Stonebridge said, folding his arms and settling in at his desk. "How is your little finger from your last expedition?"

Ed looked at his right hand. "Just a little twisted, but nothing serious."

"No pain then?"

"A twinge now and again. Certainly nothing to worry about."

"Excellent, excellent," Lord Stonebridge said. "Bit of a souvenir eh?"

"Yes sir. Very fond memories actually."

Carolyn was about to say something more serious about the damage done by the KPP terrorists in Turkey to Ed's hand during Operation Niagara, but the door opened and tea was wheeled in. They each took a cup and took their respective seat.

"I had coffee with Mr. Crowe this morning." Carolyn started the conversation, lowering her tea cup to her lap. "What he could not quite envision was how we could most effectively use our relationship with Ottawa to help us in this operation. I'm afraid I couldn't add much, since it involves relationships at such a high level."

"Good thinking, Eddie," Mr. Cooper offered. "Straight to the point and quick off the mark."

"Yes absolutely," Lord Stonebridge added. "That is the crux of the matter isn't it?" He looked about the room, judging his next words carefully. "Last night," he said, speaking louder now, "I phoned to my counterpart in Ottawa, the head of CSIS. We spoke briefly. He spoke to his boss, and phoned me back."

He stood and walked around to the front of his desk, leaning back onto it. "He confirmed we have their full support, and I stress full support, in making plans using their resources in this matter. They will not, of course, be involved in any part of the actual capturing of this man. That is our responsibility alone. Beyond that, they are one-hundred percent on-side."

While he was speaking, Ed took the opportunity to turn slightly toward Carolyn and gave her a 'thank you' wink. She replied with a very quick smile, and turned back to Lord Stonebridge."

"So," Lord Stonebridge said enthusiastically, "let's top up our tea and get down to work."

"May I start?" Carolyn asked, after they had retaken their seats.

Lord Stonebridge waved her to proceed. "Miss Andrews."

She spoke matter-of-factly. "Mr. Crowe has a Canadian passport. We will be using our contacts at CSIS to address the political issues involved. By that I mean they will travel to Libya and speak on behalf of the British government outlining specific concerns and realities of the bi-lateral relationship. Mr. Crowe is part of the Canadian team—after all he is Canadian. He is, I assume, the only addition to the team. In reality he represents MI6. His job is to find and collect the individual—details to be worked out. If he is not successful, or more to the point if he fails, or to be more blunt if he is caught—he will be persona non grata in Canada. He will likely have to give up his Canadian passport. He will be a British spy in the eyes of the Libyan government notwithstanding they will, at a very high level, be aware of his intentions. He may be imprisoned, possibly shot. Out of sight, out of mind." She paused. "Have I got it about right?"

There was a delay before anyone spoke.

"You do have a way of coming to the point, Miss Andrews," Mr. Cooper said. "I particularly like your ability to summarize the facts so succinctly. I should warn you, however, to never consider politics as a career. You are too honest by a country mile." He ended with a genuine smile.

"Thank you, General," Carolyn replied. "I accept your comments as a compliment."

They all turned to Lord Stonebridge who had been motionless during Carolyn's comments. He looked at Carolyn, nodded his understanding, and looked at Ed. "What do you think of that Mr. Crowe?"

"I'd hate to have to give up my Canadian passport, sir. I just voted in the General election. I'd feel like a traitor."

Carolyn rolled her eyes, but said nothing.

"The points you make, Miss Andrews, are extremely important," Lord Stonebridge said, looking directly at Carolyn. "Therefore we should keep them in the forefront of our minds as we work on our potential plan, recognizing that this is still all theoretical. It has not been accepted as a formal operation as yet."

"Who has final approval?" Ed asked.

"I do," Lord Stonebridge said, shrugging his shoulders. "So let's see if we can come up with a plan that I'd approve."

Four hours later they had set out a plan that all agreed was a good start. Lunch was ordered, and delivered to the patio. The setting was relaxed compared to the morning's work and it allowed each of them to take advantage of the early afternoon warmth. Ed and Carolyn sat at the table closest to the garden and Mr. Cooper and Lord Stonebridge sat closer to the French doors leading to the dining room.

"I meant it, you know." Ed said.

"What's that," Carolyn asked, taking a deep breath of the comforting air.

"I really don't want to lose my Canadian passport. I know I haven't officially earned it yet, but I do intend to take the exam; and pass."

She smiled. "I understand that, Ed. My concern was more to the possibility of your being thrown in prison. The chances of them shooting you are one in a million. They would then have the entire force of the British government down on their heads." She frowned, thinking of the international implications. "We may not rule the seas as we used to, but we are not without significant power. And we most certainly have the prime minister that has, and will, use that power."

"As in the Falklands."

"Exactly."

The food was brought to their table and they set the discussion aside while they ate.

"Done any bird watching lately?" Carolyn asked.

"Quite regularly. I've lost count of how many new birds I've identified since moving to Canada." He spoke enthusiastically. "My latest was a Pileated Woodpecker. Massive bird. Larger than a Pied Woodpecker back home."

"Home?" she asked, raising her eyebrows.

He acknowledged her question with a nod. "Picked up on that didn't you?" He sat up in his chair as if to make a point. "I learned from a fellow in the Queen's Head that I'm now allowed to have two homes:

England and Canada. He was born in Liverpool and moved to Canada fifteen years ago. Now, you see, when he is flying to England, he's flying home. But when he's flying back to Canada, he's also flying home." He paused, grinning. "I like that!"

"I can see that's very comforting. But doesn't living there for fifteen years, versus five months make a difference?"

"No, it's the mindset that counts. You have to recognize that where you live is home. Otherwise what are you? A tourist with a home and job? No, it doesn't work. My home is Canada; my home-home is England. I can choose to fit the circumstance. How can you beat that?"

"Good for you," Carolyn said. "I'm jealous of you."

"You could do the same," he added quickly.

"No," she retorted, just as quickly. "I could never think of Bulgaria as my home."

They smiled at each other, both knowing that wasn't what Ed meant. They finished their lunch and wandered back to Lord Stonebridge's office.

"So the question," Lord Stonebridge resumed, looking around the room, "is when do we get started? When can we move?"

They had taken their respective seats in Lord Stonebridge's office, refreshed and each wanting to finalize the plan.

"That depends on some measure on how quickly Ottawa can move, doesn't it?" Mr. Cooper replied.

Lord Stonebridge nodded his agreement. "Indeed it does. But the fact is their representatives are already in Malta, and are waiting for our directions. They are using Malta as a base from which to fly to Tripoli where all discussions are being held. They still have to approve their involvement in the plan, but for all intents and purposes, they are ready."

"Has Colonel Gaddafi actually been involved in the discussions?" Carolyn asked.

"Not directly," Lord Stonebridge answered. "However, the senior Canadian representative has met with him privately and has received his personal approval of our intention. But all hell will break out if we remove the man from Libya, and officially it will be an international relations disaster."

"For Mrs. Thatcher to address?" Ed asked.

"Who better?" Lord Stonebridge smiled as he spoke. "Back to the question. When can we move?"

"Is the plan approved now?" Ed asked Lord Stonebridge.

"Not until I speak with Ottawa. Assuming they have no issues, then yes it is approved. The only other step is for me to speak with the prime minister. She, of course, will neither approve nor disapprove the plan. Whatever the outcome, she will have to be in a position to state categorically that she did not approve the plan."

"Then I think we should start immediately." Ed said.

Lord Stonebridge looked at Mr. Cooper and Carolyn for their response.

"Agreed," Mr. Cooper concurred.

"Agreed," Carolyn added.

"Then it's agreed," Lord Stonebridge said, standing and walking to the front of his desk. "I'll speak to Ottawa right away, and make arrangements to speak with the prime minister tomorrow." He thought for a moment. "Let's agree to meet in my office in London tomorrow afternoon at five."

They all agreed. Ed and Mr. Cooper stood ready to move on. Carolyn remained seated.

"I have an idea," she said. "More of a suggestion actually."

Ed and Mr. Cooper sat back down. Lord Stonebridge waved her on to speak.

"I would like Ed to phone his mother today and tell her that he has to fly into London tomorrow for a meeting with the new owners of Mr. Cooper's travel agency. The meeting will be tomorrow afternoon, and he has to fly home tomorrow night." She paused, looking around. The three men nodded. "That will allow Ed to have lunch with his mother, and still have plenty of time to get to our meeting by five."

"Mr. Crowe?" Lord Stonebridge asked.

"Great," Ed said with a smile. "It's almost the truth!"

"I'll sort out the details," Mr. Cooper offered. "I'll return to London tonight."

Ed hung up the phone. "Well, is she chuffed," he grinned. "Lunch at twelve, and she absolutely understands that her world-traveling son can only stay for an hour or two."

"I'm glad," Carolyn said. "She's such a nice lady."

Ed nodded in agreement. "And she's inviting Roy Johnson. I sure hope he can make it."

Carolyn grimaced. "Oh God, I still have to get back to him about his asking me to marry him."

Ed smiled, recalling that Roy had asked Carolyn to marry him, in front of Ed and his mother, having only met Carolyn an hour before. The offer of marriage was understood to be Roy's method of both acknowledging Carolyn's charm and welcoming her into the tight-knit friendship Ed and Roy enjoyed.

"I'm sure you will decline most graciously," Ed said, bowing slightly to reflect the occasion.

"Who said I'm going to decline?" Carolyn asked, tilting her head as if pondering the question.

"I jumped to conclusions," he said, bowing again. "My apologies, madam."

She thought for a moment. "But you are correct, I must say no. My job just doesn't allow me to accept his hand in marriage." She paused. "At least not at this time." She turned on her heels, head held high, and walked onto the patio,

Ed followed her outside.

"Can we go bird watching?" he asked.

She turned smiling. "Let's do that! Before my mother knows we're free and tries to interrogate you about your intentions with her daughter."

They walked quickly onto the grass and headed up into the forest at the far end of the garden. Stonebridge Manor sat on fifty acres of land that had been in the Stonebridge family for hundreds of years. The forest, known locally as the Black Hills, was untouched by any form of human expansion. Birds and animals had it to themselves, except for the occasional visitor.

"You'll be staying for dinner, Mr. Crowe?" Lady Stonebridge called after them from the French doors.

Ed turned. "That would be my pleasure, Lady Stonebridge," he called back, waving his thanks.

Carolyn took his hand and walked faster toward the trees.

She led them through the forest, pointing out where she had played as a child with her friends. She described how as children they would play hide-and-seek in the area of the forest where the trees were taller, and the sun rarely broke through to reach the ground. She pointed out the small pond, in which they would dangle their feet and pretend there were large fish ready to attack them.

"But this is my favourite spot," Carolyn said, as they entered a small area where there were no trees. The long grass waved gently in the wind and benefited from the full warmth of the sun. She twirled several time, holding her arms outstretched. "Isn't this beautiful?" she asked. "Isn't this lovely, Ed?"

"It certainly is, Carolyn," Ed said, looking around. "You have a very lovely favourite spot."

She walked through the grass thinking back to the many hours she had spent right here in her favourite part of the forest. She looked at Ed and smiled.

"I know it sounds silly Ed," she continued, "but this is where we sat and talked about getting married."

"You and your almost-fiancé?"

"Yes. It's funny really. He never actually asked me to marry him. We just took it for granted."

"How old were you then?"

She smiled broadly. "It was my eighth birthday." She chuckled, shaking her head. "Can you imagine that? Eight-year-olds talking about getting married."

"Did it surprise him when you told him . . . whatever it was you told him?"

"That I didn't want to marry him? Yes, it did. I hurt him a lot, and I feel very bad about that."

"I can certainly understand his being hurt," Ed said. "How's he managing now?"

"He's got a new girlfriend, and rumour has it that they are soon to be married." She winked. "In this case 'rumour' being my mother!"

"That's nice then."

"Yes, very nice. At least it helps me clear my mind of it all."

She walked over to him and took his hands. "Kiss me," she whispered, moving his hands around her waist. He did as he was told. They held on to each other, not speaking, for several minutes. When they separated, she took his hands again.

"The next time we come up her, Ed, I am going to bring a blanket and we're going to make love . . . right here." She looked down at the ground as she spoke. "And I mean right here!"

"It will be my pleasure," he murmured, smiling.

"It will then officially be our special spot."

He smiled at the thought. "Shh," he said quietly, "don't make any noise, but turn around slowly and look into the ash tree."

She turned slowly, and he held her at the waist to direct her. "That," he said close to her ear and pointing into the tree, "is a Hawfinch. A very shy bird."

"I see it," she whispered. "What lovely colours."

He pulled her close to him, placing his hands over her breasts. She moved her hands over his and squeezed them gently. They stood without moving, watching the finch flit from branch to branch. It flew away without making a sound. He kissed her quickly on the neck, took her hand and they slowly headed back to the Manor.

Dinner was served in the formal dining room. Lord Stonebridge sat at the head of the table, with Lady Stonebridge to his right, and Mr. Cooper next to her. Carolyn sat to her father's left, and Ed was next to her. They took less than half of the table's length. The dinner was a three-course meal and the conversation was limited to general everyday discussions. With summer coming to an end, weather was an active topic. This led Lord Stonebridge to his annual concern of the costs of heating the Manor. Lady Stonebridge's suggestion that they move to the south of France attracted only a look of bewilderment from Lord Stonebridge, and a smile from Carolyn.

"You'll never guess what I learned from Mr. Crowe today, Mother," Carolyn changed the subject, kicking Ed under the table. He smiled, looking from Carolyn to Lady Stonebridge.

Lady Stonebridge looked at Carolyn over her glasses. "I don't like guessing my dear." She turned to Ed. "And what was it you were good enough to impart to my daughter's general knowledge today, Mr. Crowe?"

Ed was thinking furiously how to respond.

"Well, I er . . . ," he mumbled.

Carolyn kicked him under the table again. "What I learned was about the birds and the bees, Mother, and likely something you do not know."

Lady Stonebridge was taken aback. Lord Stonebridge and Mr. Cooper now turned to listen.

"More the birds actually," Carolyn explained. "I learned today what a Hawfinch looks like and further that is a very shy bird." She turned to Lord Stonebridge. "Are you aware of it being shy, Father?"

He smiled, knowingly. "Yes dear, I am. It is a lovely bird. Did you take note of its large beak?"

She nodded that she had, and went on to explain where in the forest they had seen the finch.

"Ah, your favourite spot," Lady Stonebridge said, patting her lips with her dinner napkin. "Did it bring back fond memories my dear?" She didn't wait for an answer before turning to Ed. "It is so lovely, don't you agree, Mr. Crowe?"

"Quite lovely," Ed agreed. "I can see why it would be a favourite spot. It is certainly a wonderful location for bird watching."

"I'm sure it is, Mr. Crowe," Lady Stonebridge said with a smile. "I'm just sure it is."

"You are a trouble maker," Ed said, wagging his hand at Carolyn.

Carolyn was driving him back to the Inn in her own car. He had thanked the Stonebridges for a lovely evening, and was glad that Carolyn had offered to drive him.

"Just keeping up the conversation," she replied, keeping her eyes on the road.

"I thought for a moment your mother was going to mention Paul what's-his-name."

"Reynolds, Paul Reynolds. That would be Paul Reynolds the lawyer, or barrister to be more precise. No, I don't think she would do that. Although I'm sure she was tempted."

They drove through the countryside with the car windows down, enjoying the freshness of the air. The sun had set just minutes before. Ed wondered if Carolyn's favourite spot would, by now, be taken over by rabbits, badgers, and other wildlife: perhaps an occasional fox. Certainly not bears, moose, or coyotes; which were more likely to inhabit a similar clearing in Canada's forests. He was comparing animals in his mind as Carolyn pulled up the car in front of the Inn.

"The General and I will be here tomorrow at eight a.m. sharp," Carolyn said, leaning over to kiss Ed goodnight. "Remember I love you, Ed," she reminded him, ushering him gently out of the car.

CHAPTER THREE

MONDAY, OCTOBER 1ST

•••••••

"I still think you should have phoned your mother to tell her you've invited me for lunch," Carolyn said, pulling the car over to the curb half a block from Mrs. Crowe's house. "I feel quite awkward about what you're doing."

"Trust me," Ed said. "She'll be excited about you joining us. Besides Roy will be even more surprised. This will be fun. Just go along with my story." She shook her head, expressing her concern. She put the car in gear and drove the car up to Mrs. Crowe's house.

They had driven in from the Inn, taking their time. They had four hours to get to Mr. Cooper's previous travel agency, have Mr. Cooper make the quick introductions, drive Mr. Cooper home, and make it to Ed's mother by noon. It had all gone as planned, and it was just on twelve when Ed knocked on his mother's door. He was looking forward to being 'home', to see his mother again, if only briefly, but mostly he was looking forward to seeing Roy's reaction to Carolyn joining them for lunch.

Mrs. Crowe opened the door about to ask Ed if he'd forgotten his key, but seeing Carolyn standing next to Ed completely surprised her and she was taken aback for words. She looked at Ed, turned to Carolyn and when the surprised faded she gently took Carolyn by the arm. "What a lovely surprise, Miss Andrews; do come in. How charming you look." She showed Carolyn the way. "Nice to see you too, Edwin," she added, almost as an afterthought. Ed followed them into the living room, pleased with himself.

"Roy, look who has joined us for lunch," Mrs. Crowe said, excitedly. "You keep her company Roy, and I'll add a spot at the table." She left for the kitchen.

"Why Carolyn—Miss Andrews, you have made my day!" Roy was quickly on his feet, and taking Carolyn's hand kissed it ceremoniously. He motioned her to sit in the most comfortable chair. "And you too, Eddie," he added; turning to shake hands. "How nice to see you." His grin said more than his words.

"Always a pleasure, Roy," Ed said smiling. "I phoned Carolyn just as I was getting on the plane in Toronto, and she happened to be in England. Well Bob's your uncle, she picked me up from Heathrow; and here we are!"

"Bob's your uncle indeed." Roy nodded his head knowingly. He was going to say more but Mrs. Crowe returning from the kitchen with a set of cutlery, had him postpone his comment.

Mrs. Crowe, Ed, and Roy scurried around the table, and within seconds the table was set for four.

Carolyn looked at Mrs. Crowe. "I do hope I'm not putting you out, Mrs. Crowe. I did suggest we phone you in advance, but you know how busy the traffic is?"

Mrs. Crowe waved off the apology, taking off the apron she was wearing. "Nothing makes me happier than to see you . . . except to see Edwin of course," she added, thoughtfully. "You look very nice today, Carolyn, and I just love your blouse. The color suits you so well. Now do tell us all about where you are working now. Roy and I were wondering about you, just this morning."

Carolyn outlined her job and duties in her new role in Bulgaria. She described Sofia, the capital, her day-to-day duties and the difference of living and working in a country that was in a constant state of flux both politically and financially. With her university background in European history and her current knowledge of Bulgaria, it was fifteen minutes before she realized how long she had been speaking.

"I'm sorry, I must be boring you." Carolyn ended.

"Absolutely not." Roy said.

"Oh no, it is all so fascinating," Mrs. Crowe agreed.

"Terrific stuff." Ed added.

Mrs. Crowe invited them to the table and commenced serving dinner.

"It's nothing special," she said, carrying in from the kitchen a large plate of spaghetti and meatballs. Putting the plate on the table, she looked a little sheepish. "Not very English is it?"

"We're all Europeans now, Mrs. Crowe," Carolyn replied. "It looks lovely, and I haven't had a good Italian meal for months."

"Well said," Roy said enthusiastically, "well said." He moved the serving plate in front of Carolyn to start the meal.

They ate with little conversation, except to express to the cook how wonderful the food was. Mrs. Crowe accepted the compliments with a generous smile.

"So, Edwin," Mrs. Crowe said as they finished the meal, "why don't you tell us all about Canada?" She turned at Carolyn. "Both Roy and I have visited Edwin since he moved to Oakville. He has a lovely flat. You should visit him sometime." She immediately regretted the comment, and started shuffling the plates to hide the unintended suggestion.

"I will do that sometime, Mrs. Crowe," Carolyn replied quickly. "I still have girlfriends in Toronto whom I haven't seen for some time."

All four cleared the tableware into the kitchen, and settled back around the table with a fresh pot of tea.

Ed took the opportunity to up-date everyone on his activities in Canada, in addition to the sweeping political changes taking place. "So we have a new government with a new prime minister, both less than a month old!" he said, finishing his up-date.

The conversation continued covering all topics. Mrs. Crowe enjoyed Carolyn's company tremendously; to a point of agreeing with everything she said even when, in her heart, she didn't. A fresh pot of tea helped continue the conversation that they all enjoyed.

"Well I must be off!" Roy announced, looking at his watch. "Some of us have work to do."

Carolyn stood to shake hands with Roy. "My decision is still under consideration in regards to your offer of marriage," she said. "It is indeed an important decision for me." They both understood that it was her way of expressing her friendship.

Roy grinned intensely. "You are a lovely person, Carolyn, and any man you decide to marry will be a very lucky person indeed." He kept his eyes on Carolyn as he spoke.

Mrs. Crowe tilted her head, smiling.

Ed looked away briefly, not wanting to catch Roy's attention.

Roy shook hands with Ed, thanked Mrs. Crowe again for a wonderful meal and left to return to work.

Ed and Carolyn helped Mrs. Crowe with the dishes, and explaining that he had to complete his business in London and return to Toronto that night, they left his mother waving at the door.

"Thank you for looking after Edwin on such short notice," she called after to Carolyn. "Please visit any time you're in town."

Carolyn waved back, nodding her acceptance of the invitation.

They gave their final wave, got in the car, and started the short but always-busy drive into downtown London.

Carolyn turned to face Ed. "Very nice lady."

They were stopped in the usual traffic jam that haunted London. Nothing could be done about it. It was a way of life.

"Thanks." Ed said. "Just wish I didn't have to lie to her."

Carolyn chuckled slightly. "I think it's safe to say that she'd prefer to hear a white lie rather than knowing that you might be heading off to Libya to bring back a murderer."

Ed nodded and that conversation was concluded. He turned to Carolyn. "She's certainly taken a liking to you."

"Good taste, I suppose," she replied smiling.

Ed nodded.

Carolyn looked sideways at Ed. "You don't suppose she, you know . . . that we . . . ?"

Ed shrugged. "I suspect she dreams about the possibility, yes." He took a deep breath. "But she's English enough to know that in reality those sorts of things don't often happen and when they do they rarely work out."

"I'm not sure I like that answer at all," she replied curtly. "That sounds so old fashioned."

"Okay," he said, turning in his seat to face her, "let me try this." He paused. "Have you ever been to Ascot; and by that I mean Royal Ascot? You know the one with all the hats."

Carolyn chuckled. "That's just tradition. It doesn't mean anything."

He raised his eyebrows in a questioning manner.

"Okay, so I've attended Ascot," she said in a matter-of-fact way. "It's no big deal. Just a lot of old money, most of whom wishing they had as much money as the so-called new money."

"Be that as it may the fact is the Royal Family, Ascot, and all the pageantry surrounding the British way of life is important to Mum; very important. If she knew that you were at Ascot, do you really think she would have served spaghetti?"

"I don't see why not."

"Well don't ever tell her you were there for my sake," he chuckled. "Suffice to say she knows you reside in a different world. She just doesn't know how different."

"I think you're wrong," she huffed. She drove on keeping her eyes on the road ahead. "Besides," she asked quietly, "don't you agree with the Royal Family?"

"I absolutely do," Ed said bluntly. "I like the Head of State not being a politician and deep in my heart I'm a traditionalist."

"Thank God," she said, turning to him. "I'd hate to think I've fallen for a republican!"

They drove on slowly, now passing through the trendy Chelsea area of London.

Carolyn pulled into the underground parking lot of the building that was home to the "official" headquarters of MI6, the British Secret Intelligence Service. She drove down two floors of parking and then entered a separate area that required her to show a pass. The man at the gate spoke into a microphone attached to his jacket lapel. Ed assumed he was checking Carolyn's license plate number. After a brief wait, the gate opened and the man waved the car in with a smile.

"He looks a bit old to be much of a guard." Ed wondered.

"He's a semi-retired associate. Don't let the gray hair fool you."

"Perhaps a future job for you?" Ed quipped.

"Or you?" she added.

Carolyn parked the car. They entered a lift that with Carolyn's pass took them to the fifteenth floor. A guard with a gun held directly at them welcomed them as the door slid open. Ed froze, wondering if he should raise his hands.

"Morning, Miss," the guard said, lowering the gun. "Nice to see you again."

"Good morning," Carolyn replied, recognizing the guard.

At Carolyn's direction Ed was issued a pass that included a signature, a photograph, and a fingerprint. It took only minutes.

Carolyn looked at her watch. "Perfect," she said, "we're ten minutes early."

Lord Stonebridge welcomed Ed and Carolyn to his London office. Mr. Cooper was seated and ready to start work. The office was noticeably different from his office at Stonebridge Manor. At the Manor his office was large, comfortable, well furnished, with expansive windows and a view of the grounds. His London office was large by general standards but small in comparison. The furniture was basic, leaning to uninspiring. The office was internal with no opportunity to view the skyline of the heart of London.

"Security," he explained, without having anyone ask the question.

He gestured for them to sit at the three chairs facing his desk, which they did.

"Do we have an approved operation?" Mr. Cooper asked, leaning forward.

"Indeed we do," Stonebridge replied, obviously happy that their plan had found acceptance at the highest level in London, and by the powers-that-be in Ottawa.

"Does it have a name?" Ed asked.

"Operation Hawfinch," Stonebridge replied with a slight smile.

"Very good, sir," Carolyn said. "Strong, quiet, and industrious."

"Exactly what I had in mind," Stonebridge said, nodding. He reached into his desk drawer and handed each of them a file.

"I took the opportunity this morning to document a high level summary of Operation Hawfinch. Please read through the document, and then the four of us can discuss its contents. It reads like a simple challenge, but let's not kid ourselves. We are dealing with a very problematic leader of a very complicated country."

Mr. Cooper, Carolyn, and Ed opened their files, nodding their understanding of his comments.

"You read," Stonebridge ordered. "I'll have some sandwiches and tea sent in."

"So why Malta?" Ed asked.

They had each read the document, grabbed a sandwich and a tea.

"We have had very strong ties with Malta for hundreds of years," Stonebridge replied. "That relationship has continued since their independence in 1964. English is one of their official languages. Valleta, the capital, has excellent communication and airport facilities, and it's only a short helicopter flight to Tripoli."

"Or away from Tripoli," Carolyn added.

"That too," Mr. Cooper agreed.

"And for those reasons," Stonebridge continued, "Valleta is where the Canadian delegations, who are representing us at this time, are residing. They're ready to go with the agreed-upon limitation that if things go wrong they will deny knowledge of Mr. Crowe's connection with MI6."

"When do we start, sir?" Ed asked Stonebridge.

"Where is your luggage and passport?"

Carolyn replied. "In my car, sir. In the secure parking area."

"Then we start today, if that's okay with you Mr. Crowe?"

"Yes sir. I'd like to get it going."

"Good. Further questions?"

They spent the next hour going over the plan in as much detail as they could address. The greatest concern was the process of actually getting the guard, who they simply referred to as 'the man' into the helicopter for transportation back to Malta, and eventually to London. The agreed-upon answer was reluctantly accepted by each of them.

"You will need to get firearm training right away, Mr. Crowe." Stonebridge summed up the discussion.

Ed raised his hands in reluctant acceptance. "How . . . ?"

Mr. Cooper interrupted him. "Two levels up, Eddie. Full facilities available. You need only get training on a small revolver, one you can carry on your person. They cannot, will not, search any official representative of another government. Nothing to worry about there."

"Can you expand on the details regarding the airport at Tripoli?" Carolyn asked. "It seems that is the location of the action. Are we sure 'our man' is there?"

Stonebridge opened his desk and placed an aerial photo of the airport. "This is only weeks old, so we can feel comfortable that it is accurate," he said.

They gathered around his desk.

"This," he said, pointing at the photo, "is the main terminal. Keep in mind this is not the Tripoli International airport. That would be an entirely more complex possibility. The name of this airport is Okba Ben Nafi, and has been the facility used by our Canadian representatives during the ongoing secret discussions. In the southern part of the facility are both the military air base, and the heliport. The Canadians have been using the heliport as their landing stage from Malta. The distance between the base and the heliport is no more than four hundred yards.

That is the riskiest part of the operation, getting our man from here," he pointed at the base, "to here." He pointed at the heliport.

"We're sure he's at the air base?" Carolyn asked.

"That is what we've been assured. He's a guard at the military base. His duty is guarding the hanger. And by luck, or by circumstance, he works four to midnight."

Mr. Cooper leaned into the photo adjusting his eyes to the smallest details. "Are they what I think they are?" he asked looking at Stonebridge, pointing to the military base area.

"If you're thinking they're Russian MiG fighters then you would be correct." Stonebridge replied.

"Oh my," Mr. Cooper said, rubbing his chin. "That could put the fox among the chickens!"

"Any additional risk there, sir?" Carolyn asked.

Stonebridge shook his head slowly. "Not that we can think of. The reality is the MiGs are there in the event of a U.S. strike against Libya, and the chance of that happening in the next week are nil and zero."

"We know that, sir?" Mr. Cooper asked the question carefully, fully understanding its implications.

"We know that." Stonebridge affirmed, raising his eyebrows to make the point.

They each let the confirmation sink in.

Ed assumed the prime minister had spoken to the U.S. president in order that such a clear statement could be made.

Mr. Cooper was impressed at the speed such a decision could be made, and put it down to Mrs. Thatcher's determination to get the issue resolved.

Carolyn worried if such a decision indicated a greater risk for Operation Hawfinch than she had until now anticipated.

They each kept their thoughts to themselves. Nothing was to be added by sharing these worrying thoughts.

"Then we're done!" Stonebridge said. "Let's get Mr. Crowe up to scratch on hand-held firearms."

"Not very big, is it?" Ed asked the firearms instructor.

"Nay," he replied, in a broad Scottish accent, "but it can kill, and ya die for a long time, yeah?"

Ed nodded, regretting he had made the comment. He held, with both hands, a Webley .38 caliber revolver. It was not much longer than six inches and didn't weigh more than a few pounds. The instructor put ear protection on both his and Ed's head, and motioned Ed to fire when ready.

Holding his arms straight out in front of him and with a grimace on his face pulled the trigger. The recoil wasn't enough to push him back into the instructor who stood directly behind him, but enough to drive his arms up in a jolt.

Ed looked at the target fifty feet away. He searched for the telltale hole, but could see nothing.

"Did I hit it right in the middle where the dark spot is?" Ed asked, peering.

"Ya didna hit the bloody target at all," the instructor replied, obviously with some satisfaction. "Gimme here, laddie, let ma show ya."

After two hours of practice and less than complimentary comments about the English way of life, Ed was graded as being acceptable for the job at hand. He wondered to himself if that simply meant he wouldn't be capable of shooting himself in the foot. That was now a distinct possibility, with the revolver strapped tightly to the inside of his left ankle.

"I feel not unlike a fool," Ed muttered, walking uncomfortably along The Strand with Carolyn. Lord Stonebridge and Mr. Cooper were a few steps ahead of them. They were all to dine at The Savoy. Ed was to stay the night there, and be ready to leave by five the next morning.

"Just forget you're wearing it," Carolyn laughed. "No one's going to be looking at your legs are they?"

He looked down at his legs and then across at Carolyn's. "You've got a point there," he agreed.

After a relaxed and excellent meal, Stonebridge, Mr. Cooper, and Carolyn made their way to the lobby of the hotel. A car was waiting for them. Ed shook hands with Stonebridge and Mr. Cooper and they wished him well. Little else needed saying. Carolyn had hung back, and he managed a gentlemanly hug before she headed to the car.

"Don't forget what I said at breakfast yesterday," she smiled.

"And I love you," Ed replied.

She got into the car and it pulled away slowly into the London traffic.

Never thought I would be staying at The Savoy, Ed mused to himself. If only Mum knew he thought; she'd never believe me.

CHAPTER FOUR

TUESDAY, OCTOBER 2ND

• • • • • • •

Five minutes early, Ed waited at the front door of The Savoy. It wasn't very often that he woke at four in the morning, and he now knew it wasn't a habit he wanted to get into. He'd felt almost guilty running the shower so early, knowing that the guests in the adjoining rooms would hear the plumbing. It might be The Savoy, but it was still English plumbing. He tried to compensate by packing and leaving his room quietly. Any gains he so garnered were more than offset by the lift. It sounded its age.

He had paid the bill, trying not to let his reaction to the cost of one night's stay show. Definitely to be expensed to the government he told himself, signing the credit card slip. He quickly converted and calculated. One third of his month's rent in Canada. And he had only slept until four!

A large black Vauxhall pulled into the hotel entranceway. The front passenger side window lowered. The driver looked at Ed. "Crowe for a flight?" he smiled.

Ed threw his bag in and got in the back seat.

"Sorry about that," the driver said, looking back. "You need to keep your humor at this time of the morning."

Ed smiled his response.

The car pulled into the almost empty street and headed west.

What little traffic there was headed the other way toward the city center and within twenty minutes they were on the motorway quickly leaving London.

As Ed expected, the drive took him to the airport where he had landed just two days earlier. Just before six the car pulled up to a small plane. Ed thanked the driver, got out, and entered the plane.

It was smaller than he had flown in before. The only other person on board was the pilot, who was going through a pre-flight process. He waved Ed to take any seat, and continued with his checking details. Ed took the seat behind the co-pilot seat, sat back, and waited.

After a quick introduction the pilot turned his attention to instruments, gave Ed the thumbs up, and the plane moved forward slowly.

Any thoughts that the flight would be similar to his previous flights were quickly dispelled. The plane left the ground, and almost immediately went into a forty-five degree take off. The speed and angle caught Ed completely off guard. He didn't take the opportunity to look out of the window. Instead he closed his eyes and didn't open them until the plane had leveled off, some five minutes later.

As he opened his eyes, the pilot had turned to check on him. "You okay, mate?"

Ed struggled to respond with a level of clarity. "Never better."

"I should have warned you," the pilot laughed. "When you're trained to fly in the navy, the sooner you're into air the better you feel. Taking off from carriers you see."

Ed nodded his understanding. He smiled, and swallowed to set his throat straight.

The pilot reached to the co-pilot's seat, grabbed a leather bag, and passed it back to Ed.

"Breakfast," he explained. "Okay if I fly and you serve?"

"I wouldn't have it any other way!"

After a breakfast that consisted of tea and digestive biscuits, the flying settled more smoothly. They were at forty thousand feet and on autopilot.

"I couldn't hold the plane steady at this height," the pilot explained, "so we use our little computer here." He pointed to the instrument between his and the co-pilot's seat. "We call it PFM." He paused. "That stands for Pure Fucking Magic."

"I'll have to remember that." Ed said.

The sun was full in the sky as they flew over the Mediterranean Sea. The pilot identified the countries below. "And that little spot," he said, pointing forward, "is Malta. Sit back and relax, we'll be there in less than twenty."

Ed sat back, determined to relax.

After what Ed considered to be a normal landing, a Customs officer drove to the plane, quickly stamped Ed's passport, and waved on the plane. As they taxied to a waiting cab the pilot turned to Ed. "Note the date of your entry into Malta."

Ed opened his passport. His arrival was dated September 25, 1984; five days earlier.

Ed thanked the pilot, grabbed his bag, and got into the waiting cab.

The cab ride was a short one. Fifteen minutes later the cab pulled into the grounds of The Royal Malta Golf Club and pulled up in front of the clubhouse. A tall, well-dressed man paid the cab driver as Ed got out.

"Mr. Crowe," he said, extending his hand, "welcome to Malta and welcome to The Royal Malta Golf Club. My name is Fraser, Lylle Fraser. And as the old saying goes, I'm from the government and I'm here to help you."

They shook hands.

Lylle showed Ed to his room. It was small, very basic, and looked over the eighteenth hole of the golf course. It was more than Ed had expected. Lylle suggested Ed unpack and that they meet on the members' verandah in thirty minutes.

Lylle was sitting at a table far from the entrance to the members' bar. There were two untouched glasses of beer on the table, one of which Lylle slid over to Ed as he took a seat.

"Blue Label, the local brew," Lylle said. "It's good ale. I'm told you're a beer drinker?"

Ed nodded. "Everything in moderation," he smiled, taking a drink. He returned the glass to the table "That is nice."

Lylle took a long swallow. "Moderation eh? That's your goal here in Malta . . . and beyond?"

"I hope so."

"So do I, Mr. Crowe."

"Can we go with Ed?"

"Certainly. And Lylle's fine too."

They turned to watch a four-some play through. The course was well manicured and the trees were small palms. The topography was mostly level, with well-placed valleys and mounds to offer a challenge to an average player.

"Do you play?" Lylle asked.

"Afraid not. But I've been thinking about taking it up."

"If you do, take lessons. Otherwise you'll never enjoy it."

"Thanks, I'll keep that in mind."

Lylle took another long swallow. "You're my responsibility while you're here, and I don't want you to screw anything up, okay?"

Ed nodded. "Fine by me." He paused. "Is it do-able?"

Lylle shrugged. "Not if we don't try."

Ed took comfort in the 'we' response, since it was clear that if anything went wrong it was his problem, and his alone.

"Thanks." Ed said, smiling.

They downed their beers.

"Your role here" Lylle said, now more seriously, "is that of a driver and a note taker. The driving role offers you opportunities to complete your main task, yes?"

"Okay."

"The note taking role is more important that you might think. You have to capture the essence of what you hear their interpreter say, and balance that with how you read the body language of the Libyan representative. They don't allow us to bring our own interpreter. That would be too easy for us. Understand?"

"Understood." He paused, thinking.

"What's your question?" Lylle asked.

"Well if my role is successful and we, I mean I, manage to get our man out, doesn't all of the on-going negotiations just disappear?"

Lylle nodded slowly. "Sure it might, but only for a few months. After the circumstances are argued and we all call each other names; after the television stations move on to other issues; and after the main British press move on, then we will be back here continuing the discussions. There are many very serious issues still to be addressed. Our man, as you call him, is just a blip in the process. An important blip for sure, but a blip never-the-less."

"We will return, but not me."

"Exactly. So don't screw up. And if you do, don't screw up too badly. The worse you screw up, the longer it will take to resume discussions."

"You don't sound too comfortable about the possibility of success."

Lylle grinned. "Ed, I'm a diplomat. My work is all about words; inflections of words; the order of words; sometimes very important words, sometimes no-so-important words . . . but all words. Your role is to take risks that could get yourself and perhaps others hurt. Do you understand?"

"Yes."

"Good. Then don't screw up."

"Got it!"

Lylle smiled. "Okay. I'm sure it will work out fine."

They stood and shook hands.

"I'll introduce the other two members of the team," Lylle continued, "at the members' bar for drinks and supper at six-thirty. They don't know the details of Operation Hawfinch. They've just been told you're replacing our regular driver/note-taker, and to go along with everything you do. Get some rest; we start tomorrow morning at six."

"Start?" Ed asked.

"We fly to Tripoli. That is why you're here isn't it?" He walked into the clubhouse without waiting for a response.

Ed slowly ate his Patizzi, which he had learned was a favorite dish in Malta. It consisted of a light flaky pastry filled with vegetables. It was very good. During pre-dinner drinks, Lylle had introduced Ed to the two other members of the negotiations team.

The second-in-command was Sue Banks. She was short, not much over five feet, with short dark hair. She was very professionally dressed, which set off well her slim figure. She had explained with a laugh that her role was 'bad cop', and for Ed not to be surprised at her challenging and questioning everything of importance that was discussed. 'Dog with a bone,' is how Lylle had described her, and she pleasantly accepted the comment as a compliment. Sue had a PhD from the University of Toronto, and was now living in Ottawa. Ed was tempted to ask if she knew Pat Weston, but decided against raising the possibility. Sue's thesis was on International Marketing and Distribution of Pharmaceuticals, which Ed learned later, was perfect for the negotiations being carried out in Libya.

The fourth member of the team was Mike Sampson. He was a lawyer from Winnipeg and had studied both International and Constitutional Law. He was, Lylle explained, the Canadian expert on International Treaties, and often traveled with the prime minister when his knowledge was required. Mike was older than the others, perhaps in his forties Ed thought. He was tall with a full head of dark hair and was, even in their general discussions, very articulate in his use of words.

Their discussion was general in nature, and it seemed obvious to Ed that the goal was to stay away from anything that might bring him, or his role, into the fore.

Sue and Mike made early exits with an early call in store for the morning.

"Nice people," Ed commented, shortly after they had both taken their leave.

"Very nice people." Lylle agreed. "Very professional. Both could be making considerable more money than they do in the private sector. So like I say . . ."

Ed read his thoughts. "Don't screw up. Got it."

CHAPTER FIVE

WEDNESDAY, OCTOBER 3ʳᵈ

• • • ● ● ●•• •

The helicopter took off from the golf course at six sharp. A few early golfers took the time to watch, but most were more interested in practicing their swing. The four of them were crowded in the back of the helicopter, with little room to move. Within a minute they were over the Mediterranean, and Malta was in the distance.

Ed had to shout to be heard over the engine. "It seems too small a helicopter to get us all the way to Tripoli," he commented to Lylle.

"It is." Lylle replied.

"Ah," Ed replied, hoping for an explanation.

Lylle leaned over and said, grinning slightly, "Trust me."

Ed nodded and turned to look out of the window. Sue Banks gave him a comforting look, having overheard the conversation. "You'll see," she mouthed.

A bumpy hour later, he better understood. The helicopter slowly descended and not too far in the distance was a large ship.

"Jesus, that's a massive ship," Ed exclaimed. He looked at Lylle and then to the ship. "Is that an Aircraft Carrier?"

Lylle nodded. "The Ark Royal."

Ed shook his head in amazement. "I didn't realize the Royal Navy was involved in the process."

"It isn't," Lylle said, "at least not officially."

Ed chewed his lip, thinking. "Isn't the Ark Royal new?" He asked. "Isn't it one of the Navy's most modern ships?"

"Yes," Lylle paused, "and no."

"Good, that's very helpful," Ed said, looking at Sue and Mike for help. They both smiled knowingly.

They exited the helicopter. The pilot had turned off the engine and the blades were slowing to a halt.

"He will re-fuel and be gone in ten minutes." Lylle explained.

Lylle led them to a holding room directly off the landing deck. Few of the men working around the ship took time to look at them. They were all busy doing just about every job imaginable. Painting, cleaning, plumbing: even a considerable amount of carpentry was visible—on all levels of the ship. Lylle closed the door.

"This is the Ark Royal and is it quite a ship, indeed both a beautiful and deadly ship. It is still in the process of being fitted out, and would normally be of the coast of England somewhere, certainly not off the coast of Libya. We are here at the special request of the Prime Minister, Mrs. Thatcher."

"To show the flag?" Ed asked, now understanding better.

"I'm afraid that is also a yes and no," Sue Banks added.

Ed shrugged his shoulders.

Lylle expanded. "The Ark Royal, at this time, Mr. Crowe, is not part of the Royal Navy. It will not be officially commissioned into the navy until next year. As you can see much work is being done to it. It is, however, quite capable of hitting a target as small as a house—shall we say as far away as Tripoli?"

"I'm with you," Ed said, nodding. "Showing the flag, but only unofficially?"

"Exactly," Mike said, "exactly."

"The rest of the way Mr. Crowe will be more comfortable," Lylle said, "and courtesy of the Royal Navy. Please follow me."

They walked out onto the landing area, just as a very large helicopter was raised from the level below. The pad that it was raised on stopped when it was level with the landing deck. Almost immediately the helicopter's blades starting slowly turning.

"Say hello to a Sea King, Mr. Crowe," Sue Banks said. "Now you're in for a treat."

Ed was surprised at the size of the Sea King. As the engines warmed up and the pilot and co-pilot went through their pre-flight routine, he had a chance to look around. He estimated that twenty people could be carried in comfort, thirty at a squeeze. It was big; and surprisingly less noisy than the smaller helicopter they had flown earlier. In only a few minutes, they were in the air and heading south.

"Let's go over the plans for the next few days," Lylle said as they gathered in the rear of the helicopter. "The only major difference is that Ed is replacing Miss Gisel who has flown home to Canada to look after her sick mother. So Ed will take notes and be our official driver." They all nodded in agreement.

Lylle acknowledged their understanding and continued. "The short term goal then, is to continue to reduce the conversation to two items; oil and medications. That is; we want their oil, and they want our medications. All other issues, such as their joining the World Trade Organization aren't going to happen. Sue, I'd like you to make that point clear, okay?"

"My pleasure," Sue replied.

"Mike, please continue to stress the point that governments don't manufacture medications, private companies do . . . at least where we come from!"

Mike nodded. "And money doesn't grow on trees. I'm with you, Lylle."

"That's part of the problem, of course," Lylle continued. "Their money doesn't grow on trees, but it does almost pop out of the ground in the form of oil."

"But if we, or at least the British, stop the flow of oil, then," Sue added with a frown, "they're S.O.L.!"

"Would that really happen?" Ed asked. "Would 'we' really do that?"

Lylle thought for a moment. "Let me put it this way Ed. If Mrs. Thatcher asked President Reagan to help cease the flow of oil from Libya, what do you think his answer would be?"

Ed shrugged. "I don't know. That would be pretty risky politically wouldn't it? I'm sure the American citizens don't need another oil crisis similar to the one in the seventies."

Mike responded thoughtfully. "You point is well taken Ed, but if there were ever a U.S. President that could pull it off . . . he's your man."

"Only time will tell, ladies and gentlemen," Lylle said. "But we can be sure of is this: if Mr. Crowe's operation is successful, the tensions internationally will be reduced—at least in the long term!"

"And if it isn't successful?" Sue asked, hoping for more details.

"Then we'll all be back in Canada a great deal earlier than we had planned." Mike said with little emotion. "And I'll be in a position to return to my curling league."

Sue shook her head. "Winnipeggers! You'd think winter in Winnipeg was a pleasant experience."

Mike smiled. "It's a dry cold. Besides we do get plenty of sun!"

Ed made a mental note to determine what a dry cold was.

At Lylle's direction Sue gave Ed a briefing note on Colonel Gaddafi. He started to read it slowly, and looked at Sue. "He speaks English?" Ed asked, somewhat surprised.

Sue nodded. "Read on."

Ed read further. "He trained for a while in Britain!"

"Obviously a good learner," she replied.

After Ed had read the briefing, Sue took the document and handed it to the co-pilot. "It stays on board," she explained.

"We're not expecting to meet him are we?" Ed asked.

"Not really," Sue said. "But he *is* Libya, and it is always wise to understand your opposition. The main point is that we know he detests, for lack of a better word, President Reagan. I'm sure he's no fan of Mrs. Thatcher either; but—and this is important—he does have personal ties to Britain. Dealing with us, as Canadians, is close enough to Britain without having to deal directly with representatives of Mrs. Thatcher."

"He won't confuse us with the U.S. then?"

"No, he's way too smart for that. We just don't go out of our way to bring the U.S. into any conversation."

The pilot announced they would be landing in twenty minutes.

Lylle motioned to Ed to join him at the far rear of the passenger area.

"Are you carrying anything?" Lylle asked.

"Carrying anything?" Ed replied, not understanding the question.

"Okay," Lylle whispered angrily, "do you have a God-damn gun attached to any part of you anatomy? Understand?"

Ed looked over Lylle's shoulder to see if anyone had heard. "Well yes, I suppose I do." He paused as Lylle gave him a dirty look. "Yes, yes I do," he corrected.

Lylle took a deep breath and exhaled to calm himself. "We're on the same side here, Ed, so please don't play smart-ass with me."

Ed nodded, feeling his face redden.

"I'd suggest you take it off for today." Lylle continued. "You won't be needing it, and in the unlikely event they want to search you—which you will not allow—it is always easier to tell the truth. Yes?"

"Yes . . . Thanks." He removed the revolver and holster from his ankle with Lylle doing his best to cover his actions. "I don't like wearing one of these things anyway." He was happy to hide the gun, feeling more comfortable without it.

They returned to the front of the helicopter, just as it started it's descent into Tripoli's military airport. Reaching into his bag, Ed quickly compared the photograph of the airport taken from the air, which Lord Stonebridge had given him. Nothing had changed. As expected, they were landing on the southeast end of the airport, close to the military base.

They each thanked the pilot and co-pilot, and grabbing their bags exited the helicopter. It took off as soon as they were clear. Ed watched it head west.

"It's heading to Tunisia," Mike explained to Ed. "Safer there than here."

They were in an area of the airport filled with many helicopters, and within a minute of their helicopter taking off two vehicles pulled up beside them. From the jeep in front several heavily armed guards surrounded them. Ed followed the example of his team members and stood motionless with his bag by his side.

The senior member of the soldiers looked them over individually, turned to one of his men and spoke in Arabic.

The soldier, who was clearly their translator, addressed Lylle directly. "Who is this," he asked pointing to Ed, "and where is the usual female?" His English was clear with little trace of an accent.

Lylle explained the circumstances that required Ed's attendance. The two soldiers spoke at some length. They walked around Ed silently, and then got back into the jeep.

The second vehicle was a van. As directed, the driver of the van left the engine running got into the jeep, which drove slowly away.

Lylle motioned to Ed. "You're the driver. Take it away."

"So where does our helicopter go?" Ed asked driving the van and following Lylle's directions.

"Taguermess in Tunisia. They'll be back tomorrow at 3 p.m., all thing being equal."

Lylle put a finger to his lips, motioning for them to be careful what they say. "Very friendly people here." He added, grinning. "Pull up over in front of that building, Ed."

He was pointing to a one-story brick building that was typical of many buildings at any airport. It was built for function, not for looks.

"This is your new home-away-from home, Ed," Sue said as the van stopped and Ed turned off the engine. The interior was considerably more modern. The center of the building had been converted into a boardroom. There was a separate kitchen to the right, a fully equipped bathroom to the left, and five doors leading to separate bedrooms in between.

"Can you cook, Ed?" Sue asked.

"I can do a mean Greek dish," Ed replied with a smile.

"Then you're chef for tonight," Lylle said. "Make up your list of ingredients. It'll be the first item on the agenda."

"When do we begin?" Ed asked. He was beginning to feel both excited and nervous.

Lylle looked at his watch. "In exactly twenty-seven minutes, at nine o'clock. And I mean exactly nine o'clock. Remember these are military; flexibility is not a word they understand."

They each selected a bedroom, grabbed their materials, and were sitting at the boardroom table at eight fifty-five. Lylle sat at the head of the table at one end, Mike and Sue sat on either side to him, and Ed sat next to Mike. The table could seat twelve. Plenty of room for 'them', Ed thought. He had written out the ingredients for tonight's meal and left it at the far end of the table from Lylle. He settled in his seat, wrote the date on the top of his note pad sat back, and waited.

At nine o'clock four men entered the room. They acknowledged their guests with a quick nod of their heads. No other introductions or pleasantries were made. Ed recognized two of the men from earlier, the interpreter and the senior officer. The third man simply took the sheet of ingredients and left the room.

The fourth man was obviously the ranking officer. His uniform was more highly decorated, and his shoulder epaulets bore four stars. Ed assumed he was the equivalent of a four star general. He spoke quietly to the interpreter and faced his guests as the message was passed on.

"General Shalgam would like to talk about the World Trade Organization today." The interpreter said with a shallow but gentle smile.

"While your citizens die of Hepatitis A?" Sue interjected. She spoke quickly and sharply.

The interpreter looked slightly shocked at the quick response and took his time to convey Sue's comments.

General Shalgam listened, not taking his eyes off his guests. When the message was completed he did not respond. He slowly made direct eye contact with each of them, showing no emotion. He nodded his head slowly, and then spoke at some length in Arabic.

The interpreter eyed the General carefully, and then spoke. "You are representing a government that seems to be more worried about our population than it does about the citizens of Ireland who are, as you know, killing each other over the capitalistic interference by the same government that you represent."

The room fell silent. No one turned to look at Lylle, but each knew he was the only person that could respond.

When Lylle replied, he maintained a clear and crisp voice. "Unfortunately General Shalgam it is true that there are differences of opinions in the governance of Eire and Northern Ireland as, indeed, there are in many countries. Few countries are fortunate to escape the inequities of history. Unlike your own, however, other countries endeavor to resolve such differences through political freedom, the freedom of speech, and—if sometimes annoying—the freedom of the press. Such is not the case in your country. So let me make it clear that neither the government we represent nor your four guests here today need lessons in human rights."

The translator re-organized his notes several times and spoke slowly and carefully to ensure accuracy of translation. When he was finished he turned away from the general and back to his notebook.

If the room was silent before, it was now uncomfortably silent. Ed could hear himself breathe and wanted to hold his breath in the event everyone else could hear him.

General Shalgam looked directly at Lylle for what appeared to be minutes. He finally turned to the translator and spoke briefly. The interpreter spoke as if nothing had been said before. "The general wonders what your agenda might include for today's discussion."

Mike responded appropriately and quickly. "Our hope, General Shalgam, is that we could address the relationship between the continued delivery of petroleum products to your customers and the potential of reducing the cost of medications through mass purchasing of those medications most needed by you government." He distributed a sheet of paper to each person at the table. "These are some of my notes on the issue and as you will see the government we represent is most willing to negotiate with the pharmaceutical manufacturers on your behalf."

Ed felt he was in the midst of some true diplomats and was amazed at the turn of events in just a matter of minutes. He, Lylle, Sue, and Mike kept their comments to themselves and shuffled their papers during the translation of both Mike's comments and notes. None of them wanted to express, or appear to express, any level of success of the meeting thus far.

The interpreter coughed to get their attention. "General Shalgam approves the items for discussion. With your approval we will take fifteen minutes to review Mr. Sampson's comments in more detail, and in the meantime I will arrange for coffee to be delivered." Without waiting for any form of agreement, the three soldiers left the room closing the door quietly as they left.

Ed looked around, waiting for direction. Mike was expressionless. Sue smiled. Lylle gestured to Ed "Have you taken any notes yet?"

Ed shook his head. "No I haven't. I confess I was distracted." He quickly put pen to paper.

"And what do your notes now say?" Mike asked.

Ed looked at each of them. "They say the meeting started at nine am, and we agreed upon an agenda." He shrugged. "That's it!"

"Very good, Ed," Lylle smiled. "You'll make a good diplomat."

"Well done, sir," Sue said to Lylle.

Ed raised his hand, pointing to the ceiling. "Aren't we worried about . . . ?" He didn't finish the sentence.

"Not now, Ed." Lylle said, shaking his head. "Diplomats don't tape diplomats, at least not when they are unsure what might be said. A tape recording catches all conversations, not just those words that are to your advantage. We all learned something from the Nixon White House tapes."

"But the van?"

"They weren't in the van, were they?" Mike added. "Besides it's just a van, not a formal gathering. Honor amongst thieves if you will, but if we don't all play the game the same way nothing would get done. Now where's that coffee?"

The meeting re-convened at ten o'clock, everyone having had as much coffee as they needed. As awkward as the need for translation made the conversation, the discussions appeared to Ed to be moving slowly, but positively, to some sort of resolution. Agreement was reached to work through lunch, with few having any real appetite. It was apparent to Ed that with the discussions going as well as they were, no one wanted to disrupt the pace. He took notes, keeping them at a high level and stressing the agreed-upon issues, making only passing comments to those issues that remained un-resolved. The meeting ended at five pm, with little acknowledgment of the day's progress. The soldiers left quickly and without fanfare. Ten minutes later the ingredients for their evening meal were delivered. While Ed worried over supper, the four reviewed the day's activities while standing in the kitchen area. Ed listened more than he spoke. It was agreed it had been a good day and that tomorrow should allow specific and important details to be sorted out. No reference was made to the seemingly confrontational beginning of the meeting.

The table was set and the four enjoyed a relaxing and well deserved Greek meal. Ed had cooked his one and only meal; de-boned chicken breasts stuffed with feta cheese and spinach, and served with Greek-style potatoes. The others were impressed, but he kept it to himself that it was the only full meal he was capable of producing. The discussion during supper was strictly personal and few questions were addressed to Ed. His exact role was not fully understood, and the least known the less trouble they could get themselves into.

Ed retired early to his room. He reviewed again in considerable detail the photograph of the airport, and spent some time looking at the photograph of 'our man'. Feeling relatively comfortable with the operation so far, he went to bed rested and relaxed. Almost too relaxed he suspected.

CHAPTER SIX

THURSDAY, OCTOBER 4TH

•••••••

Ed was up and dressed before the others. He walked outside of the building. It was six-thirty and already warm. The sun was just over the horizon. To his right was the end of the airport with an iron fence about two hundred feet away. To his left was the full extent of the airport. The east-west runway was two hundred feet ahead of him. He turned to his left. This was the area he was most interested in. Along the distance of the runway were a variety of buildings and holding areas. It was in one of these buildings that he had to find and capture the murderer.

He heard the vehicle some time before it pulled up in front of him. Immediately upon stopping, a soldier jumped out and motioned him back into the building. Ed nodded his understanding, while taking a deep breath and motioning to the clear blue sky.

"Lovely day," he commented, smiling at the soldier.

The soldier agreed with a nod pointing to the building to make his message clear.

Ed gestured drinking with his hands, smiling. "Coffee?" he asked.

The soldier nodded his understanding, and gently took Ed by the arm and turned him toward the building. Ed followed the instructions and went back into the building.

As he entered Lylle stood back from the window, shaking his head.

"Well, did you set us back a day by pushing your luck?" Lylle asked.

"Just ordering coffee," Ed smiled. "It's a chef's job."

"Coffee is delivered every day at seven am," Lylle said, going back to the window to look out. "I'll put this oversight down to my error this time, but please don't jeopardize either your role or ours by assuming this is some kind of holiday camp."

Ed accepted the comment with a nod. He looked around to ensure neither Mike nor Sue was in listening distance. "When do you think I might be in a position to take my next step?"

"Not this trip." Lylle said. "We head back tonight to Malta, and we'll come back again on Saturday. I'll drag out the negotiations today, with the intent of coming to an agreement I am not in a position to personally approve. Hence we fly back tonight, and return on Saturday morning to convey our superiors' approval but with a couple of caveats. That will allow us to work until late Saturday night. That will be your opportunity. One opportunity: one time. Hit or miss, that'll be it. We fly out of here Saturday at the agreed-upon time." He emphasized the next comment. "That will be with you—or without you. Is that clear?"

"Very clear, and thanks. I do understand the potential risks I am making for each of you. I'll do everything to ensure your safety."

Lylle waved good-morning to Sue as she walked from the bathroom to her bedroom. "Coffee's on its way," he called. He turned to Ed. "I know you will."

The meeting started at exactly nine o'clock. There was little ceremony, and no general chatter. The discussion related to the importation of medications appeared to be going well, but was taken off track many times with Mike making references to international agreements and organizations, some of which Ed had not heard of before. References to the IBRD, IMO, WCO, and many others had the Libyan delegation scrambling to translate and understand the intricate interrelations of one to the others.

The afternoon session started smoothly; only then did Lylle, Mike, and Sue disagree on what level of authority they had as a group to conclude the business of the day. While they agreed and disagreed on the details of their level of approval, General Shalgam shook his head and watched with a look of disbelief.

As Ed had been expecting from Lylle's comments, agreement on medications was agreed-upon with the limitation that the agreement was tentative until approved by Lylle's superiors. It was agreed, with Ed's greater respect for his associates' capabilities, they would all re-convene on Saturday morning to finalize this important agreement.

Before leaving the building General Shalgam spoke through his translator with his final comment for the day.

"The General wants you to know that he has found this to be a frustrating couple of days, and hopes the meeting on Saturday will be less complex." The translator looked up to ensure his message was clear. After receiving acknowledgement from his four guests, he continued. "Further General Shalgam wants you to know that your helicopter has received approval to land, and will be here in an hour."

Lylle nodded his thanks. "Please convey our thanks to General Shalgam," Lylle said, "and let him know that we also would like to finalize this as soon as possible." He paused. "Could you ask the general if we could tour this most beautiful airport in the short time we have before our flight is due to leave?"

The translator, somewhat taken aback by the request, conveyed the request.

General Shalgam thought about it briefly, and with a broad smile and laugh replied.

The translator, now smiling, relayed the message. "The general says that will be fine, but please do not get out of your van; and the Russian MiG 25 Foxbats you are searching for are at the south end of the airport."

General Shalgam left quickly with a slight bow, and a hearty laugh. Having quickly documented their notes and packed the four gathered around the board table.

"Good work, everyone," Lylle said smiling. "Mike, remind me not to go up against you in court. Well done."

"Thanks," Mike said, somewhat embarrassed by the compliment.

Sue put her hand on his shoulder, and quoted nicely. "Lawyers, I suppose, were children once: Charles Lamb."

"But not for long," Mike replied. He turned to Lylle. "What's the plan regarding the airport. Do we know they have Russian planes here?"

"Absolutely we do, but its good that's what they think we want to confirm," Lylle said. "But in reality I want to get a layout of the buildings on the airport grounds, and taking a turn around as we head to the heliport will allow us to do that."

"And have a peek at the MiGs as we do it," Sue added.

'Yes," Lylle said with a smile. "And when we get close to them we'll take our time and drive slowly. That'll convince them that's what we're up to."

Shortly after the Sea King had taken off they compared notes on what they had each captured. Between their scribbled notes and Sue's sketches they pulled together a map of the buildings in relation to the landing strips. Ed compared the results to the photograph from Lord Stonebridge.

"Excellent," Ed said. "My sincere thanks."

The remaining trip back to Malta was relaxed and the conversation limited to the success of their trip.

"But let's not forget Saturday," Lylle reminded them. "That's the big day for the agreement . . . and whatever else things have in store for us."

CHAPTER SEVEN

FRIDAY, OCTOBER 5TH

• • • • • • •

"So it used to be a U.S. Air Force Base?" Ed asked.

He was sitting with Lylle and Commodore Paul Duke of the Royal Navy. They were sitting on the golf course patio, comparing the photo of the airport with the drawing that had been pulled together the day before.

Commodore Duke nodded. He was dressed in his summer uniform and wore the almost mandatory well-kept beard. "Since 1943, when it was captured by the British Army, until January 1970 it was Wheelus Air Base. Basically a stop-over for attacking the USSR in the 60's so it was, and still is, very strategic from a military perspective."

"And what do our friends in Washington have to offer as advice," Lylle asked.

"If, as we have been told, our man is guarding the Russian warheads, then Washington believes he is working in one of these two buildings," the Commodore said, pointing to the photo. "Or buildings 17 or 18 on your diagram. The actual Tu22 bombers are located in these hangers." He pointed again at the photo. "So it would make sense that the bombs be stored in 17 or 18." He shrugged. "It's certainly where the US Air Force kept theirs!"

"Right next to the heliport." Ed said, wondering if it was a co-incidence or a well-planned convenience by the Libyan authorities.

"Too damned convenient for my liking," Lylle added. "You'd think they wanted us to get him!"

Ed didn't look up from the diagram.

Commodore Duke smiled quickly and shrugged. "Sometimes these things work out for us, yes?"

"Maybe," Lylle answered. "What do I know? I'm just a civil servant."

"Aren't we all eventually?" the Commodore asked, getting up to leave. "Good luck gentlemen. I'll see you on the Ark Royal tomorrow." He saluted, and left.

Ed spent the rest of the day practicing his marksmanship with his pistol. The Royal Malta Golf Club was part of the Marisa Sports Club, which had its own shooting range. He was not overly pleased with the result of his target practice, but had learned how to more quickly remove the pistol from its holster on his ankle, and how to return it to its holster quickly and safely.

The four ate their evening meal on the patio of the golf club, overlooking the 18th hole. There was no discussion of tomorrow's events.

They turned in early; having agreed that leaving at six in the morning would allow enough time for them to sort out the remaining details of the agreement. Nothing was said of Ed's operation.

CHAPTER EIGHT

SATURDAY, OCTOBER 6TH

• • • ● ● ● • •

The helicopter rose quickly, and the early golfers took little time to watch it, preferring to spend more time on their game. It was exactly six o'clock. Ed had joined Lylle, Mike, and Sue for a quick coffee, preferring to spend as much time as he could in his room to ensure his holster and pistol were correctly and firmly attached to his left leg. He once more reviewed the photo of the man he was after. It was blurry at best, but he drilled into his head what the man looked like . . . and what he had done.

Lylle had raised his eyebrows in a questioning manner as Ed joined them at the table, and Ed had nodded—barely moving his head—to confirm that he was now armed. Lylle, having drained his cup of coffee, wished them all a good day's work, and left for the helicopter. Ed, Mike, and Sue followed suit by draining their coffees and followed Lylle to the helicopter.

Just prior to stepping into the helicopter, Sue had gently touched Ed's arm to hold him back. "I hope you have a successful day, Ed," she said. He nodded his thanks and they entered the helicopter.

The Sea King was ready for them as they landed on The Ark Royal. As they were walking to the Sea King with their bags, Commodore Paul Duke waved Ed over. As they met, they turned their backs to the noise of the larger helicopter. The Commodore spoke close to Ed's ear. "We received confirmation that our man is working the four to midnight shift today." He shook Ed's hand. "Good luck." He saluted with a quick smile.

"Thank you, sir," Ed replied, half saluting but not quite sure if it was protocol. He turned and walking against the draft from the propellers joined the others on the Sea King.

Their van was ready for them when they arrived. There was no greeting party. The van sat on the runway with the keys in the ignition. As he drove the short distance to the building where the meeting was to be held, Ed took a quick look at buildings 17 and 18. They did not appear different than any other of the buildings surrounding the airfield. They had doors large enough to allow small planes to enter and exit and he estimated they could hold four or five small planes each. There were regular people doors on both side of each building. The only obvious difference was that there were no windows on the buildings themselves, or on any of the doors. He drove on to their meeting building and did not look back as they parked the van and entered the building.

Coffee was available and they each helped themselves. Ed looked at his watch. It was eight forty-five.

At exactly nine o'clock General Shalgam and his interpreter entered the room. The general acknowledged their presence briefly and sat at the head of the table. He spoke through his interpreter. "General Shalgam assumes we can finalize the details of the agreement by noon, and you can quickly be on your way home."

Lylle removed some papers from his bag. "There are a couple of problems yet to be resolved I am afraid, but no doubt we can work them out amicably." He smiled at the general.

The general was aware from Lylle's response there was a problem before the interpreter had translated, and he was visibly annoyed. He spoke through the interpreter, banging his fist on the table as he did.

"The general is not amused by this delay, and wants to cancel the meeting immediately."

"Hear us out General Shalgam," Lylle said, raising both his voice and his hand. "There are some problems to be addressed, but I think we can get you more medication than we had discussed earlier this week."

The message was well received, and the interpreter asked Lylle to expand on the issues to be addressed.

The discussions went as expected by Ed. Lylle, Sue, and Mike often argued amongst themselves as to what they could reasonably offer in price and speed of delivery of the medications. The volume was not as issue. Lylle had explained they could guarantee fifteen percent more than had been discussed earlier. The increase in volume was a top priority for General Shalgam, and Lylle knew that as long as that guarantee was not discussed further, the general would continue the discussions.

It was visibly frustrating for the general. His goal was to secure the medication so needed in his country. While the price and delivery time were important, the volume was a priority. He was looking forward to reporting to his senior officers of the increase in volume he had negotiated. It would be good news, very good news. Good for the country but perhaps better for his career advancement.

The discussions regarding medications ended shortly after lunch to the great satisfaction of General Shalgam. The negotiations moved onto the matters over which the general had some control the price, and distribution of oil. Without the sale of oil Libya was not only short of medications it was short of funds, especially foreign currency. The current sale of oil to its Arab neighbors was not enough to keep the country's finances in an acceptable situation. In fact, unknown in any detail outside of Libya, the country was close to bankruptcy. Oil was its only export, the lifeblood of the nation.

Negotiating an agreement with the United Kingdom was a significant goal, not for direct sales of oil to the United Kingdom; this was a small percentage of Libya's exports. What was important was the indirect result of the agreement: the resumption of oil exports to Libya's two largest customers, Italy and Germany. They represented over seventy percent of oil exports. They represented financial life or death. This agreement was the answer to many prayers, and General Shalgam was aware of his place in his country's history. He would not fail; could not fail.

Lylle started the negotiations by offering ninety percent of the current OPEC approved price of petroleum, commencing January 1st 1985.

Ed thought General Shalgam was going to have a heart attack. His verbal response was initially controlled but got louder and more exaggerated as he continued. It ended with his fists thumping the table in exasperation, and his gesticulation that the meeting was as good as over. While the translator took the time to translate into English, none was necessary. The parameters had been set; now only some acceptable mid-point had to be agreed upon.

Ed took notes as the negotiations continued, but his mind was on the goal of having the meeting extend beyond four p.m., and his thoughts on successfully transporting the killer from the hanger to the Sea King.

Lylle, Mike, and Sue had no problem in meeting the first goal. By four-thirty the agreement was complete. But to the general's frustration and to Ed's considerable admiration, Lylle insisted on going over the main items of the agreement one more time to ensure there was complete understanding. Lylle addressed each item slowly and deliberately, with Sue and Mike nodding and agreeing with the details as documented. When everything was finalized, the general shook hands with each of them and left quickly to convey his success to his fellow officers. It was now six-thirty and getting dark. The sun was slowly setting below the mountains far into the west.

They took their time in getting ready to leave, and slowly walked to the van. No one was there to guard or protect them. They were no risk. They were, today anyway, friendly foreigners.

Ed drove slowly across the airfield toward the heliport. They could see their Sea King. It was parked in the second closest spot to buildings 17 and 18.

"Well," Lylle said, "that was a good day. In twenty minutes the engines will be warmed up to fly us home to a nice glass of beer!" He nodded to Ed as he spoke. Twenty minutes. Ed was sure that would be enough time. The area around the Sea King was quiet as they parked the van and walked with their bags to the open door. Sue and Mike got in. Lylle turned to Ed. "Twenty minutes, twenty-five at most. After that we have to leave." They shook hands. "Good luck. See you in twenty."

"Thanks," Ed said. "See you in twenty." He looked around, making sure they were not being watched. Keeping close to one side of the Sea King, he walked into the darkness.

Keeping as low as he could without slowing his pace, he headed to building 18. He approached from the side, noticing a door toward the front of the building. The only outside light was on the front of the building. He felt comfortable he would not be seen unless someone was actively looking for him. Behind him he could hear the Sea King engines very slowly warm up. The pilot was taking his time, and Ed knew he needed every available moment.

He reached the building and pressed himself against it, now looking back toward the Sea King. Nothing. He was nervous and had to convince himself to relax. He calmed down, but now he needed to pee. He was annoyed at himself for not taking advantage of the washroom after the meeting. To his own embarrassment he turned to the building and, for what seemed like forever, he peed. The engines were getting louder. He knew he had to move quickly.

He was about to move to the side door when a man behind him shouted a command. It was in Arabic, but the message was clear. He raised his hands and keeping them straight up slowly turned to face the man.

The man was dressed in a dark uniform and the only lightness seemed to be from the whites of his eyes. What Ed was concerned about, however, was the submachine gun that was pointing directly at him. Keeping his hands well up in the air, he gestured toward the helicopter, and looked down at where he had peed. He tried smiling; giving the message he had run over to relieve himself and was due back on the helicopter.

The man shook his head, motioning Ed to the side door with his gun. The door was not locked. Ed entered with the man following him inside. Once inside, the man flicked on an overhead light. It took several seconds for Ed's eyes to adjust to the brightness but in an instant he knew that the guard standing in front of him, with a submachine gun trained squarely on his head, was his man: his goal. He immediately recognized the guard's features from the photos taken at the Libyan embassy. There was no mistake. His man was ten feet away, but it was not Ed who had the upper hand. Ed motioned again to the noise of the revving engines, but the guard was not buying it. He shook his head to make that clear.

Ed slowly lowered his hands, having received the guard's reluctant nod of approval. The guard slowly switched the gun from his right hand to his left hand, and with his right hand selected a walkie-talkie from his belt. He spoke briefly into the mouthpiece, and waited for a response. The guard spoke more loudly, seemingly arguing with the person on the other end. The argument continued, and his frustration was evident. Ed pointed again to the revving engines, shrugging in innocence as he did. The guard turned slightly away from Ed to keep his attention on his conversation. Without fully knowing what he was doing, Ed seamlessly reached down to his ankle pulled out his handgun aimed and fired at the guard. The guard turned to face Ed, lifting his gun as he turned. The bullet hit the submachine gun, causing the guard to drop it. It rattled to the ground, and for a moment they both stood looking at each other.

The guard moved to recover his gun. Ed waved his handgun threateningly, making sure the guard understood he would not be so lucky next time. The guard stood still grinning at Ed, motioning to the walkie-talkie. He spoke in Arabic. His message was clear. Help was on its way.

Taking a deep breath, Ed waved his gun and pointed the guard to the door, and ultimately to the revving engines. The guard simply shook his head, grinning even more.

Time was running out. Ed knew that. He had to move and move fast. He aimed the gun at the guard's arm and pulled the trigger. The bullet hit its mark. The guard was surprised by the shot, and quickly grabbed his left arm with his right hand. He turned to Ed, obviously in pain. His grin didn't change. Ed waved the gun again, threatening to shoot again. The guard stood straight up, almost to attention. It was then that Ed saw the guard now held a large knife in his hand. He pointed it toward Ed, his face a mixture of hate and pain.

Pointing the gun to the guard's head, Ed again waved toward the sound of the helicopter, which now sounded to be running at full strength. Time was running out and it was only a matter of minutes before the helicopter had to leave.

Ed waved his gun threatening to shoot again. In an instant, and before Ed had time to react, the guard turned the blade of the knife and thrust the knife deep into his own body toward his heart. He stood staring at Ed for two seconds, and then collapsed. He landed on his side. Blood oozed from his body across the cement floor.

Outside Ed could hear the Sea King lift off, and the sound of vehicles arriving. He quickly put his gun into his ankle holster, took two steps back, and waited.

As the sound of voices got louder, he looked at his watch. It had been thirty-two minutes since he had left the Sea King. They had waited longer than they should have. He raised his hands above his head and took a deep breath—Operation Hawfinch: not accomplished.

The door burst open and quickly there were four soldiers in the building. Two went to the fallen guard, checking his pulse and listening for breath. Ed knew there would be neither. The third guard picked up the walkie-talkie and spoke quickly and urgently into it. The fourth soldier, seeing the circumstance, took his revolver from his holster, held it against Ed's head, and screamed directly into Ed's face. Ed closed his eyes, waiting for the sound of his death. A second soldier put his gun to Ed's head and among the entire racket the sound of his releasing the safety catch was loud in Ed's ear. The conversation between the soldiers was in Arabic, loud and frantic. The guns to his head were jabbed several times to ensure he knew they were ready to shoot.

The conversations quickly came to a halt as the sound of others entering the building brought them to a silence. Ed kept his eyes closed, not wanting to challenge his captors in any way. The new voice in the room spoke clearly and slowly. Ed immediately recognized it as General Shalgam. The general spoke further and the two guns moved away from his head. There was some arguing, but the general's authority carried weight.

Slowly opening his eyes, Ed saw the general taking in the scene of the events who then spoke to the soldiers while pointing to the guard. Their response was obvious—the guard was dead, and Ed had killed him. General Shalgam raised his hand to lower the tone, turned to face Ed; and showed absolutely no outward sign of recognition. Ed swallowed slowly and said nothing.

General Shalgam sent two of the soldiers out of the building in order to bring a calmer presence to the situation. He spoke into the walkie-talkie at some length, looking at the dead guard and then to Ed as he spoke. When he was finished, he put his hands behind his back and stood straight. He could have been watching a march-past of his soldiers. No expression, no words. He was going to wait. They were all going to wait.

Twenty minutes past and Ed was sure his arms were going to fail him. He had lowered them slightly, but kept them well in the air. He was tempted to motion if he could lower them to his side, but intuitively thought it would not be wise to have the soldiers see any level of discussion between himself and General Shalgam. He tried thinking of anything to keep his mind off his aching arms.

The sound of a helicopter brought the general and the two soldiers to attention. By the sound of its engines it landed only feet way from the door. The engine was turned off, but before the sound had lowered the door opened and three soldiers entered the building.

Colonel Gaddafi returned the salutes, spoke quickly to General Shalgam, and then looked about the room. He barely looked at Ed, staring intently on the dead guard. He turned to the two original guards, shook their hands, spoke to each of them and they both left the building. The two soldiers, whom Ed assumed were his personal bodyguards, remained, along with General Shalgam.

"You killed my guard," Colonel Gaddafi said, looking from the body to Ed.

"No, sir, I did not." Ed replied.

"You shot him."

"Yes, I did shoot him, but I did not kill him."

"He stabbed himself? Am I to believe that?"

Ed nodded.

"Why would he kill himself?" Gaddafi asked. "Could it have been that you were going to kill him, and like a good soldier he would rather die at his own hand than be killed by the enemy?"

Ed was reluctant to respond, not sure of what was appropriate the circumstances. He looked at the two soldiers, and then to Gaddafi.

Gaddafi spoke to Ed. "Do you speak Arabic?"

"No, sir."

"Then why do you suspect my soldiers speak English?"

"Well, I er . . ." but was interrupted by Gaddafi.

"These soldiers would die for me; they would most certainly kill for me. Do you understand?"

"Yes, sir."

"And are you willing to die for your country?" Gaddafi asked.

"I hadn't thought about that," Ed said swallowing. "But I certainly wasn't thinking of doing so any time soon."

"And do you still have a gun?"

"Yes I do."

"And no doubt it is a Webley .38, and no doubt it is holstered to your ankle. Is that correct?"

"Yes . . . to both that is."

Gaddafi spoke to his guards, and then turned to Ed. "Lower your hands, but do so slowly and carefully. Do not," he added wryly, "offer them an opportunity to get revenge for murder."

Ed lowered his hands as slowly as he could, although the pain was numbing.

Gaddafi spoke to the soldiers who quickly gathered a table and a chair. Gaddafi sat in the chair and rested his arms on the table, facing

Ed. General Shalgam stood directly behind Gaddafi and the two soldiers stood either side of the table,

"What am I to do with you?" Gaddafi wondered, taking out his side arm and resting it on the table. Ed shrugged slightly.

"Do you not have a point of view?" Gaddafi asked.

"I thought the question was rhetorical," Ed said.

"It was not."

"You could send me home. Put this all down to a most unfortunate set of circumstances." Ed mumbled, more than spoke.

"No that I cannot do." Gaddafi said, rubbing his chin. "But first, would you like a cup of coffee? It has been a long day, no doubt."

"Yes, yes please," Ed replied, surprised at the question.

Gaddafi spoke to General Shalgam, who immediately left the building.

Gaddafi continued looking at Ed, shaking his head. He spoke briefly to the soldiers who nodded or shook their heads in response. They appeared reluctant to actually speak to their leader. Gaddafi turned back to Ed.

"You seem rather young and inexperienced to kill anyone. Is the British Secret Service recruiting yuppies now?" He smirked as he spoke.

"I'm not a member of the British Secret Service." Ed replied.

"No, of course you're not. I forgot. You're a Canadian citizen assisting in an international treaty of oil and pharmaceuticals; is that correct?"

"Yes, sir,"

"As you wish," Gaddafi shrugged. "Either way, you're in deep trouble. Can we agree on that?"

"That seems to describe the situation very well," Ed said, "very well indeed."

"Perhaps what you might call an understatement?" Gaddafi asked.

"Perhaps, yes." Ed tried to smile, but could not quite manage it. He knew he was in over his head. Gaddafi was acting the gentleman, but Ed was fully aware that he was reputed to support terrorists, and was implicated in the 1972 Olympic massacre in Munich.

The door opened and General Shalgam entered with several new soldiers. At his direction they put the dead guard into a body bag, cleaned up most of the blood, and left the building taking the body with them.

"Coffee is on its way." Gaddafi said.

The coffee arrived shortly and was placed on the table. Gaddafi poured a cup for himself and General Shalgam. They each took a sip, no doubt Ed assumed to show it was not poisoned in any way.

"Help yourself," Gaddafi said to Ed, indicating to the coffee. "Fear not, if I intend to kill you, I will have no problem in shooting you."

Ed walked forward poured himself a coffee, added cream, and stepped back. The coffee was very hot and very good. He tried desperately to think of how to remedy the situation he was in. It seemed impossible. He had, in the minds of the guard's fellow soldiers, killed one of their own. He had to be punished. Gaddafi was in a bind, and Ed had put him there.

Gaddafi and General Shalgam drank their coffee and talked as if nothing had happened. Ed did not like this. They had to have a plan in mind. Drinking coffee was not the answer.

Ed couldn't think clearly. His thoughts were not working together. He felt weak at the knees and had to grip the coffee cup to stop it from spilling.

Gaddafi stood and faced Ed. "I regret that you must officially die," he said coldly, picking up his gun from the table. He aimed it at Ed and released the safety catch.

Ed wanted to run, wanted to speak, to scream, but couldn't. His body wasn't responding. He gripped the coffee cup as if gripping to life itself. He looked at Gaddafi, and saw double. His eyes were running. Perspiration ran down his back.

The last thing he saw was Gaddafi pulling the trigger. He felt the bullet hit him; felt the warmth of the blood on his skin. He closed his eyes. Everything felt ghostly; everything went black.

Commodore Duke was listening to Lylle Fraser give an explanation of what happened. Sue Banks and Mike Sampson added to the details. The three of them were distraught and spoke at the same time. They were standing on the deck of the Ark Royal. The Sea King had been stowed below and the smaller helicopter for transporting them to Malta was close by, the pilot waiting for instructions. The commodore listened, nodding and shaking his head as he heard the story.

"Well you had to leave," he said firmly. "To have stayed would have been foolish, unacceptable, and totally against orders."

"But what about . . ." Sue started, but was unable to finish the question.

"Shit," Lylle said, "shit, shit shit!"

"Let's be careful what we assume," Mike offered calmly. "We don't know what happened. I suggest we head back tomorrow . . ." but he was interrupted by a sailor running to the commodore. The sailor had on a set of earphones and a microphone. He saluted as he spoke.

"Sir, we have a helicopter coming in from Libya. Enemy target, sir."

"How far?" Commodore Duke asked.

"Fifteen miles sir."

"Go to action stations on all CIWS's immediately, but do not open fire unless I give a direct order."

"Yes, sir." The sailor repeated the command into the microphone.

The commodore moved them back against the wall of the ship. The sailor stood next to the commodore, and looked at his watch. "I would guess about ten minutes, sir."

"So would I, sailor, so would I."

A siren could be heard below and above them.

"Action stations ready, sir." The sailor said.

"Good. Let's wait and see what we've got." The commodore ordered.

"CIWS's, commodore?" Lylle asked to break the silence.

"Close-In Weapons Systems," Commodore Duke replied.

The sailor raised his hand. "News, sir," he said, listening carefully with one hand on his earphones. He looked at the commodore with a strange look. "Sir, the incoming is turning around and coming in backwards."

"That's good," the commodore said. "That is very good. Get medical staff up here right away." He paused. "Just in case."

The Libyan helicopter came in slowly, with its rear to the ship. It landed and immediately the side door opened. General Shalgam jumped onto the deck. Two soldiers followed him. None of them wore side arms or weapons. Commodore Duke walked over to the general, telling everyone else to stay back.

They saluted each other and shook hands. General Shalgam pointed to the helicopter. The two soldiers reached in and slowly brought out a body bag. They laid it on the deck. Without waiting for orders, members of the medical staff ran to the helicopter picked up the body bag and carried it back.

No one touched the bag until Commodore Duke returned, and the helicopter was heading back to Libya. The commodore nodded to the medical staff. They unzipped the bag. Ed's body was carefully wrapped to keep his arms from slipping.

"Jesus Christ," Lylle shouted. "Jesus fucking Christ."

The medical staff lowered the zipper. On top of Ed's body was an envelope, which was passed to Commodore Duke. He looked at it and shook his head. He showed it to everyone.

It was addressed in bold printing: Mrs. Thatcher, Prime Minister.

CHAPTER NINE

MONDAY, OCTOBER 8TH

• • • • • • •

She woke immediately as her phone rang. Robin jumped off the bed and left the room.

"Pat Weston," she answered succinctly.

"Pat, it's Carolyn. I'm phoning from London." She paused for recognition. They hadn't spoken by phone before. "I'm afraid I've got some bad news."

Pat sat up straighter, hung her head and closed her eyes; expecting the worst.

"Please don't tell me he's dead for God's sake." Her voice was barely above a whisper.

"No, he's not dead, Pat," Carolyn spoke quietly. "But he is in hospital, and I hate to tell you this, he's in a coma."

"Oh God almighty! What happened? How is he? Is he going to, to . . . survive?"

"Pat. Why don't you get comfortable? I know it's only five-thirty in the morning over there. Get comfortable and let me tell you what we do know. Then I'll try and answer any questions you have, okay?"

Pat stood out of the bed. "That would be fine, thanks. Let me go to the kitchen and settle in. Hang on."

She threw on her housecoat, rushed to the kitchen and picked up the wireless handset.

"Okay, Carolyn, go ahead. This is a secure line, so feel free. And excuse the noise, I'm making some tea."

Carolyn smiled at the other end of the line. She waited until the initial noises of water running and pots banging ended.

"Okay, fire away," Pat grabbed a paper and pen as she sat down.

Carolyn outlined in detail everything they knew for sure which, she explained, was not very much after Ed had left the Sea King to find and bring back the guard.

"How bad is the wound?" Pat asked.

"Not bad at all, in fact the doctors have indicated that is the least of his problems."

"Brilliant; as he would say," Pat replied.

"It's the drug that was administered that's creating the problem. The forensic people are having a problem in determining exactly what it is."

"And therefore don't know how to treat it," Pat shook her head.

"I'm afraid that's right."

Neither spoke for a while.

Pat broke the silence. "I feel devastated about this, Carolyn. I recommended him for this operation, and now he's, he's . . . I don't even know what to say he is for Christ's sake." She covered the phone, but not before Carolyn heard her start to cry.

"He assumed you recommended him, Pat. He was fully aware of the situation. We can't take it personally, can we?" She paused briefly, not believing her own comment. "I was his co-sponsor, so I share your thoughts. Believe me; everyone over here is shaken up by this." She took a breath. "To make things worse, we can't tell his mother. She thinks he's plugging away in Oakville sending his clients around the world."

"What a screw up," Pat gasped.

Carolyn did not respond.

"Are you still there?" Pat asked.

"Yes I'm still here," Carolyn said, sitting up in her chair. "Look there is one more thing I can tell you, but you must promise not to repeat it. Your people in Ottawa will not be updated on this; direct instructions from our prime minister."

"Are you sure you want to tell me? I don't want you to get into trouble."

"Just promise me, okay?"

"Yes, of course I promise. Thanks for you trust."

Carolyn spoke closer into the phone. "Well the fact is we're not really sure the operation was a loss. Inside the body bag that Ed arrived in . . ."

"Oh God . . ."

Carolyn continued. "Inside was an envelope addressed to Prime Minister Thatcher. It was delivered un-opened to Mrs. Thatcher . . . after the usual security stuff . . ."

"Go on, go on!" Pat urged.

"In the envelope was a photograph of the man we were after, and he was dead. He had been hanged!"

"Hanged?"

"Hanged; as in hanging from a rafter."

"Good God! You're not trying to tell me that Ed hanged the guy? He wouldn't do that . . . probably couldn't do that."

"We're sure it's our man, and we're pretty positive he's dead."

"Now that is gory," Pat said, pulling a face. "That's gross."

"One other thing," Carolyn added.

"I'm not sure I want to know any more. Does it get worse?"

"Not really. It's just that two shots had been fired from Ed's gun, and the gun was in its holster on his ankle."

Pat frowned. "Hey this is getting weirder and weirder. I find it hard to believe he would even use the gun in the first place. Christ, he's a bloody bird watcher."

Carolyn smiled at comment. "Yes, that's why it's Operation Hawfinch."

Pat thought for a while. "Can I ask you how you know all of this Carolyn? It's got to be top secret."

"It is, Pat. And the reason I know is because first I'm his co-sponsor, and second—because my father is commonly know as 'C'."

"Your dad's the head of British Secret Service! Wow, that takes the cake."

"Please keep this to yourself, Pat. Just between us girls as it were?"

Pat managed to find a smile. "Never a word, Carolyn. You can count on me."

"Thanks Pat. Look I've go to go, but I promise to keep you updated on any news, okay?"

Pat thought for a moment, and made a quick decision. "Carolyn. Can I tell you something I've never told anyone else? My secret to you so-to-speak."

"Please do. I promise to keep it to myself." She smiled at the thought.

Pat took a deep breath. "I love the guy. Ed that is."

Carolyn almost dropped the phone and had to make sure her voice didn't break. "Oh Pat, that is nice. I didn't know that," she swallowed hard. "Now I'm really glad I phoned you."

"No reason you would know, Carolyn. Even he doesn't know." She sighed loudly. "Of course he doesn't love me. I know that. Never will. But I wanted you to know. If for no other reason, I want you to know how much your phoning means to me."

"Well I'm glad I did, and I will keep in touch. Bye, Pat."

"Bye, Carolyn. Thanks again."

Carolyn put down the phone and put her head in her hands. She needed to think.

Pat put down the phone and finished making tea. As she sat down, Robin jumped onto her lap, purring. She hugged him. "Don't worry, big guy, you're my number one man. Ed's okay, but we're the 'A' team." As if he understood, Robin purred louder.

CHAPTER TEN

TUESDAY, OCTOBER 9TH

• • • • • •

He saw himself playing on the swings in Queen's Park. His mum was sitting talking to neighbors and watching him. Now he was at school raising his hand to answer a math question. He always knew the answer to math questions. The teacher was pointing to him, but it didn't make sense. She was calling him "Mr. Crowe, Mr. Crowe . . . . How are you Mr. Crowe?"

He opened his eyes with a fright. He hurt. His body hurt, his head ached, and his mouth was wide open with something forced down his throat. He blinked tears away from his eyes and as best he could he shook his head. It hurt; everything hurt.

"How are you, Mr. Crowe? Are you awake, Mr. Crowe?" The nurse gently held his hand to comfort him. His eyes were wide open now. The nurse's smile came into focus. "Relax, Mr. Crowe, I'll ring the doctor. He'll be here a in a minute or two."

Ed moved his eyes from side to side, trying to determine where he was. He had an I.V. in each arm, and his mouth was jammed open by the tube that hurt the back of his mouth and his throat. He looked at the nurse in terror, begging her with his eyes to remove the tube. She nodded her understanding. She removed the tape from his face holding the tube, and slowly withdrew the tube from his mouth.

"There, I'm sure that feels better," she smiled. "Not the nicest way to eat is it now?" She had an Irish accent, and an Irish smile. He felt comforted.

He tried to speak but couldn't. She reached over and gave him a pad of paper and a pen. He quickly wrote on it and turned the pad for her to read.

She read the note and understood. "Let me check with the doctor when he gets here. I'm sure I can get you some water soon."

He nodded and sat up a little higher in the bed. He looked around the room and gestured to the nurse.

"You're in hospital. Great Ormond Street hospital in London."

He shook his head. It didn't make sense. Great Ormond Street was a hospital for children. Why would he be there? He thought back to what he remembered. It was a blur, but he recalled being shot by Colonel Gaddafi, and then nothing. It seemed a long time ago. He looked down and touched his left side. The pain was still there and he could feel the bandages beneath his pajamas. He had to be careful. He had to think clearly. Was he still in Libya? It didn't make any sense. He recalled that Gaddafi said he had to die. No, something was wrong. He thought he must have been dreaming.

The nurse could see his confusion. "Just a minute, Mr. Crowe, let me get the general."

So he was still in Libya. General Shalgam was here. It made no sense. He closed his eyes in despair.

"Good morning, Eddie, my boy." Ed looked up. It was Mr. Cooper. A wave of relief relaxed his entire body. "Nice to have you back in the real world," Mr. Cooper said.

Ed nodded and grinned. It was nice to be back in the real world. Ed pointed to his throat and gagged a high-pitched, "Hi."

Mr. Cooper waved him off from speaking. He pointed to the pad of paper and pen. Ed wrote on it and showed it to Mr. Cooper, who smiled and showed it to the nurse. She gave Ed a bit of a look and turned away.

The door opened and the doctor entered the room. He spoke quickly to the nurse, introduced himself as Doctor Smith, and quickly used a stethoscope on Ed's heart and lungs.

Doctor Smith took Ed's hand to read his pulse. "So how you doing, Mr. Crowe? You've had a good sleep these past couple of days."

Ed pointed to his throat.

"He has a very dry throat," the nurse said.

"In fact," added Mr. Cooper, picking up the pad of paper, "his throat feels like, and I quote here, 'like the inside of a Turkish wrestler's jock strap'. End of quote."

"Hmm," the doctor said. "And what do you recommend, nurse?"

"Let me see," she said authoritatively, "I would prescribe a glass of water and a reduced level of imagination."

Doctor Smith nodded. "Well let's start with the water shall we. I'm not sure the management of one's imagination is covered under the National Health Service."

Ed drank three glasses of water and managed a weak, "Thank you" to the nurse.

After removing the two IVs from his arms, the nurse and doctor left.

Mr. Cooper carried a chair over to the side of the bed and sat. "I'll tell you what we know and you can fill in the blanks. We will need to do it again for Lord Stonebridge, but let's see what we can figure out."

Ed nodded, leaned back into the pillow, and listened.

Mr. Cooper relayed the details of the helicopter bringing back Ed in a body bag, the fact that it was close to being shot down, and that General Shalgam was the senior officer in charge. "We will need to work out who fits where in all of this," Mr. Cooper said. "The fact that we have received word from Libya to continue the negotiations for pharmaceuticals and oil makes it difficult to sort out. They contacted us as if nothing had happened. The negotiations team goes back to Libya in two weeks to sign the deal." He shook his head and shrugged. "We are very pleasantly surprised."

"Amazing," Ed squeaked.

"So you spent a day in Malta," Mr. Cooper continued, "and then were flown back here for specialist treatment."

"At Great Ormand Street? I thought it was only for kids."

"Let's say mostly for kids. This is a special ward for the Service. Where better to keep a sick adult secreted than in a children's hospital? It's not used often, but it works. And before you ask, the doctor's name is certainly not Smith. I don't know what it is but it isn't Smith."

"This is all a little amazing," Ed said, shaking his head.

Mr. Cooper thought for a while, and moved in closer to the bed. "So our man is dead, correct?"

"I'm afraid so. I know that wasn't the goal." Ed shrugged.

"So tell me," Mr. Cooper asked quietly, "how did you hang him?"

Ed's sat up straight. "Hang him? I didn't even kill him!" His throat hurt. He gulped another glass of water. "Jesus, where did that come from?"

Mr. Cooper explained about the photograph. "We somehow assumed, as strange as it sounds, that you hanged him. It didn't make any sense, especially when two shots had been fired from your gun." He sat back in the chair. "Tell me what happened, Eddie. You talk, and I'll keep the water coming."

Ed outlined what had happened after he had left the Sea King in as much detail as possible. Mr. Cooper listened intently without saying a word.

Ed summed up. "So the bottom line is that he killed himself; committed suicide. I did shoot him, but that didn't kill him." He thought for a moment. "You know what's unusual in all of this? Gaddafi shot me in the same place as I shot our man. Now that's scary."

Mr. Cooper closed his eyes briefly to take it all in. He smiled. "You had to take a pee?"

"Hey, I don't have to tell that part to Lord Stonebridge do I?" Ed asked. "God, I'd sound like a bloody fool."

Mr. Cooper chuckled. "You only have to tell him once. No one else need know."

"You won't tell anybody?"

"Not a soul," Mr. Cooper said, smiling. "Scout's honor."

Ed rubbed his chin thoughtfully. "So where do we go from here? By the way, what day is it?"

"It's Tuesday, Eddie, so like the doc said, you've had a good sleep. We head out to Stonebridge Manor tomorrow and you give a complete report to Lord Stonebridge. We then need to get you back to Canada, so we've arranged for you to fly back to Ottawa on Friday. The negotiation team has been asking after you. I'll let them know you're okay this afternoon."

"Thanks, Mr. Cooper. I'll rest up tomorrow and be ready to go. Incidentally, do you know where Carolyn is?"

"She's back in Sofia, Eddie. She was standing right here yesterday, but she felt she had to get back to work. This whole thing has been a strain on everyone."

They shook hands. Mr. Cooper left. Ed closed his eyes, thinking about the results of Operation Hawfinch. Two minutes later he was asleep.

CHAPTER ELEVEN

WEDNESDAY, OCTOBER 10TH

• • • ● ● ● • •

"I feel rather nervous about meeting Lord Stonebridge," Ed said, looking out of the limousine window as they passed through the gates of Stonebridge Manor.

"Why would that be?" asked Mr. Cooper. "Is there something you haven't told me? Dear God, don't tell me you did hang the man!"

"No, nothing like that. It's just that the operation didn't work out very well did it? I mean I was supposed to bring him back to justice, not have him commit suicide. Then I did get myself caught didn't I?"

"Don't be too hard on yourself. Just be thankful the crew of the Ark Royal didn't blow you and the Libyan helicopter out of the sky. Then you would be dead, dead, and not just 'officially' dead—as Colonel Gaddafi so nicely put it."

"True," Ed mused.

"Besides if you were dead, we'd have never found out what happened over there would we? No, on balance I think it's good you're still alive and he's dead. Much cleaner. Easier report for us to write to the P.M. that's for sure."

Ed turned to look at Mr. Cooper who was smiling broadly. "Well you have to consider all angles you know." He laughed aloud and slapped Ed on the back as they got out of the car. "Besides," he whispered, "Lady Stonebridge wants a chat before you meet the old man."

Before Ed had time to respond, the door to Stonebridge Manor opened, and Lady Stonebridge welcomed them in.

"You're looking fine today, General," she said to Mr. Cooper. "And, Mr. Crowe," she said turning to Ed, "you look even worse than the last time I saw you."

Ed bowed slightly. "Thank you, Lady Stonebridge, how nice of you to say so. It is a lovely day, and I do so enjoy visiting Stonebridge Manor."

Lady Stonebridge waved Mr. Cooper up the stairs to see Lord Stonebridge and escorted Ed into the large living room. Without asking, she poured tea for each of them. "No sugar, correct?"

"Yes, Ma'am. Thank you for remembering." He took his tea and sat down.

Lady Stonebridge put her cup down and turned to Ed. "Tell me honestly how you are, Mr. Crowe. You do not look well at all."

Ed nodded, accepting her seriousness. "I have a wound from a small caliber bullet, which I am told will heal perfectly. I am still weary from some sort of drug that was administered to me, and I have lost a few pounds. But in total I am on the mend, as they say, and looking forward to going home."

Lady Stonebridge smiled. "Well said. I am glad to hear that. My husband has been very worried about you, as have other members of the family."

"I'll ensure Lord Stonebridge is aware of my mending health."

"My daughter asked me to deliver this letter to you Mr. Crowe. She could not be here herself." The letter was on the table in front of her. She picked it up and walked it over to Ed. "She sends her best wishes, of course."

Ed took the envelope and putting it in his jacket pocket, excused himself for his meeting with Lord Stonebridge. He turned as he got to the door. "I did mean it when I said I enjoyed visiting your home, Lady Stonebridge."

"Thank you," she replied. "You are always a welcome visitor Mr. Crowe. You are a good friend of the family."

Ed walked up the stairs to meet Lord Stonebridge, not sure of what had just happened. He shrugged it off, tapped on Lord Stonebridge's office door, and entered.

Lord Stonebridge got up from his desk and walked around it to shake Ed's hand. "Mr. Crowe, how wonderful to see you." He motioned Ed to take a seat in front of the desk. "We have been very worried about you. How are you feeling?"

Ed recalled Lady Stonebridge's comments. "I am feeling better every day, Lord Stonebridge, and am looking forward to returning home to Canada."

Lord Stonebridge rubbed his hands with pleasure. "Excellent, Mr. Crowe. Excellent. Tea has been ordered and we have the rest of the day to sift through all of these confusing pieces of information to determine exactly what did and did not happen."

"And put Operation Hawfinch to nest, so to speak," Mr. Cooper added.

"Perfectly put, General," Lord Stonebridge said, happy at the thought. "And as our U.S. cousins would say," he added, looking toward Ed, "the Hawfinch has landed!"

Ed was surprised at their positive approach to the results of the operation. It may not have failed, he realized, but certainly did not meet its goals. The man, 'our man', was dead. He was not a prisoner to be tried for murder and attempted murder.

The tea was wheeled into the room. They all helped themselves and took their seats for the review.

Lord Stonebridge motioned to Ed. "Please proceed, Mr. Crowe. The floor is all yours. Take us through the steps one at a time, and we'll save our questions until the end."

Ed covered the details slowly and methodically, starting from when he left the other members of the negotiation team. He did not endeavor to put things into perspective of what he had learned from Mr. Cooper two days earlier, but simply outlined the actions that occurred.

"And I woke up in Great Ormand Street hospital with a deadly sore throat and two IVs of medication; one in each arm." Ed ended the story with a shrug, paused for a second and then added, "So I'm not so sure it was a very successful ending."

"Luckily," Lord Stonebridge said slowly, "that decision is mine. I certainly haven't jumped to that conclusion, and I can assure you neither has the prime minister. I think it's fair to say she is very accepting of the end result, perhaps a bit too so I might add." He chewed his lip on that thought. "Let us now review what we know happened between your dying, as it were, and your waking up in hospital, but before we do that, I do have two questions."

Ed waved him on.

"Do I take it you assume, as I do, that the cream contained whatever the drug was that resulted in your death-like status?"

"Absolutely, sir. Particularly since General Shalgam was aware that I took cream in my coffee. He had seen me pour myself coffee several times during the two meetings."

"My wife keeps telling me not to drink the stuff," Mr. Cooper added with a grin. "Although in my case she is concerned about it keeping me awake."

"Indeed," Lord Stonebridge agreed. "Now my second question is a bit, shall we say, deeper?" He looked through his notes, found what he was looking for, and looked at Ed over his glasses with concern. "You had to take a pee?"

Ed rolled his eyes. "Oh God. Stupid or what?"

Mr. Cooper laughed aloud. "Hey, who knows Eddie? If he hadn't caught you with your pants down, metaphorically speaking that is, he may have simply shot you in the back."

"It's not what happens in the spy novels though is it?" Ed asked, looking at both of them humbly.

"Nothing happens like it does in the spy novels," Lord Stonebridge said contemplatively. "I wish it did. Life would be so much easier."

They topped up their tea and returned to their seats.

"So where does this leave us, General?" Lord Stonebridge asked.

Mr. Cooper rubbed his chin, put his teacup on the desk, and sat backing his seat. "Well here's how I see it, and I've been thinking about this since Tuesday. We wanted our man, and they knew it. They were willing to let us have a go at him; bring him back to London that is. As it turned out, he died. No doubt in their official records, he was killed by a foreigner. The un-named foreigner was later killed by them and the body disposed of: probably thrown into the sea." He shrugged and continued. "Officially it had nothing to do with the negotiations. They continue as before. They get the medications. We get the oil flowing. And at a reasonable price I might add." He shrugged again. "Makes sense to me!"

"Sounds too good to me," Ed commented.

"Perhaps it does, Mr. Crowe," Lord Stonebridge said, reaching into his desk drawer and placing a newspaper on his desk, "or perhaps not." He pointed to the newspaper. "Read this."

Ed and Mr. Cooper looked at the newspaper. It was in Arabic. They only thing they recognized was a photo of Colonel Gaddafi on the front page. They both smiled at Lord Stonebridge.

"This," Lord Stonebridge said smugly, "is yesterday's copy of the Tripoli newspaper. Completely controlled by the government, of course, but in this instance that's a good thing. What it outlines is basically what you surmised General, except it makes it clear that the guard was a national hero, and Colonel Gaddafi killed the intruder personally. It goes on to say that the killer was a member of the CIA, and that his body has been returned to the United States via the British navy."

"The CIA?" Ed gasped. "Where do they fit into this?"

"They don't of course," chuckled Mr. Cooper. "But they get blamed for everything else; why not blame them for this? Brilliant, just bloody brilliant!"

"Brilliant indeed," Lord Stonebridge agreed. "In this instance Plan B worked out better than Plan A."

"Won't the CIA deny it?" Ed asked.

"Of course they will. They will deny it emphatically," Mr. Cooper said, still smiling. "And in this case they will be correct. But what does Libya care about their denials. The relationship between the two countries could hardly be worse. This won't even be a blip on the screen!"

Lord Stonebridge spoke into his intercom. "More tea please. We are celebrating!"

The tea was delivered and they each topped up their cups with steaming hot tea and helped themselves to the biscuits that came with the tea.

"To a very successful Operation Hawfinch," Lord Stonebridge offered, raising his cup in celebration. Ed and Mr. Cooper raised their cups likewise. It turned out to be a short celebration.

A man entered the room, looking visibly shaken. "I need to see you outside, sir," he said to Lord Stonebridge. "And you too, General."

They both quickly left, certain something was terribly wrong.

Ed sat for a few moments, not sure what he should do. He decided to read Carolyn's letter, not sure if it was written before the news arrived that he was out of the coma.

The letter was typed.

Dear Ed
I have been thinking about our relationship . . .

He didn't finish the sentence, the message was already clear. He moved to the second paragraph.

I have subsequently had time to reflect on our discussions . . .

He closed his eyes. This was not what he had expected. He folded the letter, not wanting to read further. He chewed on his lip, deciding to keep going. He moved to the final paragraph.

I hope you have a wonderful life . . .

He read no more, but glanced at the signature. It was signed:

Carolyn Stonebridge

Not even Carolyn Andrews, the only name he ever considered her to be. He folded the letter, put it back in the envelope, and slid it back into his inside jacket pocket. His mind was numb. Perhaps this explained Lady Stonebridge's cooler welcome he wondered. His mind snapped back into reality as Lord Stonebridge and Mr. Cooper entered the room in a rush. They were both in an obvious state of confusion. They sat down, capable of only shaking their heads.

"Mr. Crowe," Lord Stonebridge mustered, "my daughter . . ." But Mr. Cooper interrupted him.

"Terrible news, Eddie. Lord Stonebridge's daughter, Carolyn, has been kidnapped." He stammered briefly then regained his strength. "Apparently she was kidnapped at the Sofia Airport when she arrived there Tuesday. She was not expected at work yesterday, but the British Embassy received a letter today demanding one million dollars for the return of 'Lord and Lady Stonebridge's only daughter.'"

Lord Stonebridge groaned as the words were spoken.

Mr. Cooper continued. "I'm sorry to have to tell you like this, Eddie. I know you get along well with Carolyn."

Ed's heart sank. It didn't seem possible. The world wasn't supposed to work like this. To be so happy one moment and desperate for the world to be making sense few minutes later wasn't reality. It was television; actors, make-up artists; not real people. Not Carolyn, please God not Carolyn!

Ed turned to Mr. Cooper, not wanting to even appear to be addressing Lord Stonebridge. "What happens now?" he asked quietly. "What do we do?"

Mr. Cooper motioned for himself and Ed to leave the room. They excused themselves, but Lord Stonebridge did not react—could not react.

They stood aside from the door and away from the office.

"We think we have no alternative but to pay the ransom." Mr. Cooper shook his head as he spoke. "We don't think this is any kind of organized military or government plot. That makes no sense. On the other hand, we cannot be sure of the police. Bulgaria thrives on corruption. It's a way of life, always has been." He turned and looked out of the window. "I only pray to God that whoever has her is not aware of Lord Stonebridge's position in the government."

"Oh shit," Ed groaned. "Surely they mustn't know. Wouldn't the ransom be higher?"

"We think so, yes. So we want to get the money, get over there, and pay the money as quickly as possible."

"They don't have the money available? Surely? This is the British government for crying out loud."

"No Eddie, they don't have the money. No embassy sits around with cash like that. And if they tried to withdraw it within the Bulgarian banking system, every bell in the country would be ringing. No we have to take the cash from here."

Ed calmed his thinking. "Who is delivering . . . ?"

"I am," Mr. Cooper said. "As soon as we get the money, which is being pulled together in London as we speak."

"I must go with you, please," Ed begged as he clutched Mr. Cooper's arm.

"Not possible I'm afraid. The letter was clear that only one person delivers the money, and they can't be totally stupid since they insist that it be an older man."

Ed grasped Mr. Cooper's arm more firmly. "I don't need to be there when the money is delivered, but let me be there when Carolyn is released. I know she knows you Mr. Cooper but . . . but . . . God, I need to be there."

"I'm sorry Eddie . . ."

Ed let go of Mr. Cooper's arm turned and walked quickly back to Lord Stonebridge's office. He opened the door, entered, and closed the door behind him. Mr. Cooper started to follow him but stopped at the door. He went back to looking vacantly out of the window.

When the door opened several minutes later, Lord Stonebridge waved Mr. Cooper back into the office. He struggled to speak. "Take him with you, General. He makes a good point. If he can help in making Carolyn feel comfortable, it can only help." Lord Stonebridge spoke more clearly now. "Perhaps we need his luck." He stood erect, sniffing back a tear. "Lady Stonebridge and I have full confidence in your abilities. Thank you both."

Mr. Cooper nodded at Ed. "I agree sir. We do work well together."

Ed and Mr. Cooper left Stonebridge Manor heading to the airfield where they were to be met by a government representative who had the ransom money. They didn't speak during the drive. There did not seem much to say. The cloud was moving in from the west, and rain was imminent.

By the time they arrived at the airport, thrown their equipment in the luggage compartment and entered the plane, it was raining steadily. They waited for the money. The weather was miserable, they were miserable, and the plane was cold and damp. There would be no heat until the plane started its engines. The pilot explained that there was just enough fuel to get them to Sofia without re-fueling, so they had to wait.

"Spring is nicer," Mr. Cooper mused.

"Autumn is nice in Canada," Ed added. "Nice change in color of the trees."

They waited. Finally the sound of a car stopping got their attention. The sound of a car door closing led to a tall well-dressed man entering the plane. He wore a heavy raincoat, which was drenched in the short distance from the car to the plane.

"Pretty bloody awful weather we're having don't you think?" The man asked. It wasn't really a question, and no answer was offered.

He didn't introduce himself. He looked at Mr. Cooper. "You're the General I assume." Mr. Cooper nodded. The man unlocked a chain attached to his wrist and to the briefcase he was carrying. "One million dollars," he said, speaking as if he did this every day. Mr. Cooper thanked him and took the briefcase.

"By the way," the man added, "there is also a body-wire and ear-piece in the case. Direct order from the old lady. Good luck gentlemen." He left the plane. The co-pilot closed the door, and the engine was started.

The flight through the heavy clouds was bumpy and uncomfortable. After clearing the cloud the blue sky and sun made matters at least seem a little warmer. They moved to the back of the plane, and sat at a small table.

Mr. Cooper lifted the briefcase onto the table, placing his hands on it. He spoke quietly;

"Once more unto the breach, dear friends, once more:"

Ed cringed. Mr. Cooper was not normally so dramatic. Ed quoted the second line:

"Or close the wall up with our English dead."

"Well I wouldn't want to go that far," Mr. Cooper said.

"Nor me," Ed agreed. "But can you tell me what the plans are, or what we know and don't know?"

"Quite simple actually. Tomorrow a second letter will be delivered to our Embassy in Sofia with instructions on where and when to drop the money."

"And collect Carolyn?"

"Yes," Mr. Cooper agreed, "and collect Carolyn."

"You don't sound very positive about the plan. Is there something you have not, or cannot, tell me?"

Mr. Cooper shook his head. "Not this time, Eddie. You know as much, or as little, as I do. I just feel uncomfortable about the entire process. Whoever did this knows who she is, and who her father is. While it's not a state secret, she does go by the name of Andrews for a reason." He thought momentarily. "No, there is more to this than meets the eye. We just don't know what it is."

Ed understood his concern. "I'm a bit fearful to ask this, but how is Lady Stonebridge?"

"A wreck I'm afraid. A total wreck."

"Do you think she'll pull through?"

"Oh, I'm pretty sure of that. But I wouldn't want to be in the Lord's shoes when it's all over."

Ed choked at the thought. "No, neither would I."

Ed made coffee, delivered two cups to the cockpit, and returned to the table.

"So why the body-wire?" Ed asked

Mr. Cooper smiled. "Thought you'd notice that. It is SOP, as in Standard Operating Procedure, that when an operative has to attend a meeting such as what I will be doing tomorrow, the question has to be addressed as to whether or not a wire is worn. The earpiece is to be worn by a second operative in order to know what's going down and to intervene if, and when, required. So the first question is whether it is safe to do so. If the answer is yes, then it's worn."

"And the second question?"

"The second question is who the 'earpiece' is and what are the rules."

"And the fact that 'the old lady' gave a direct order for one to be delivered?"

Mr. Cooper rolled his eyes. "That would be the prime minister's direct recommendation that one be worn. Recommendation only mind you."

"That sounds a tad like a mandatory option," Ed said.

"Probably, but let's see what we're up against."

After staring at the sight of a million dollars in cash, and each pondering how they would spend such an amount, they moved to regular seats to relax and enjoy, as comfortably as they could, a flight they both much preferred not be needed. Ed was tempted to re-read Carolyn's letter, but decided not to. His need to help her far exceeded his concern and deep disappointment he felt having briefly read her letter. It wasn't the first 'Dear John' letter he had ever received, but he knew no other could ever affect him as he was by Carolyn's. Thinking of the time they had met and spent in Ankara gave him cause to smile. "We'll always have Ankara," he said quietly, wanting to put on a positive face.

"What was that?" Mr. Cooper asked, turning to face him.

"Nothing, Mr. Cooper. Just mumbling to myself."

"Gotta watch that in our business, my boy. Walls have ears you know."

Ed nodded his understanding. Point well taken he thought.

Three hours later they arrived at Sofia airport. The plane taxied away from the main terminal and came to a stop only a few yards from an exit gate. It was evident diplomatic activity had been extensive locally.

Their passports were reviewed and stamped without them leaving the plane, and there was no need to have their luggage checked. The official activities were over in less than two minutes. As Ed and Mr. Cooper gathered their bags a limousine entered the gates and drew up beside them.

The driver walked over to Mr. Cooper. "British Embassy, sir; Jack Williams," he said. He had a strong Scottish accent. They shook hands and Mr. Cooper introduced Ed. As soon as they and the bags were in the car, they left through the gate.

"We're right downtown, gentlemen," Williams said, looking back, "so enjoy the ride and the beautiful city of Sofia."

Ed and Mr. Cooper were impressed with the city. It was wonderfully clean, the traffic was light compared to most cities, and the buildings were immense and impressive.

"It is lovely," Mr. Cooper noted, obviously surprised at the architecture and the number of parks. "There seems to be a number of statues and buildings named after Vasil Levski, should we know who he is, Mr. Williams?"

The driver replied, keeping his eyes on the road. "Please call me Jack, and yes that would be a wise thing. Vasil Levski was the leader of the Revolutionary Central Committee in the 1860's, fighting against the Ottoman Empire. He is revered here. He was born Vasil Kunchev, but by popular demand he was re-named Levski; which simply translated means 'lion like'. Untimely he was caught and hanged by the Ottomans, but as you noticed his name continues."

"Thank you, Jack," Mr. Cooper said. "You never know what may come in handy in this sort of situation."

They continued driving through the broad streets, until the driver turned right and drove down several back lanes and alleys. The car came to a stop. The driver put the car in neutral and turned to face Ed and Mr. Cooper. "At the risk of being over-dramatic gentlemen, I think it would be wise if only the General be visible when we pull into the Embassy grounds. I have no doubt the Embassy is being watched."

Mr. Cooper agreed. "Good point, Jack." He turned to Ed. "Into the boot with you, Eddie. I trust you don't mind."

"I won't say it's my pleasure, but duty must and all." Ed got out as the driver released the boot lid. "But it is called a trunk to be correct gentlemen; we are driving in a Cadillac after all." He closed the door, got into the trunk of the car with their luggage, and the lid closed slowly and locked. The driver and Mr. Cooper exchanged smiles, and continued on the journey.

The ride was comfortable enough for Ed although the darkness was depressing. He reminded himself that he was hugging a million dollars in cash. It didn't make it any brighter, but he at least knew he had a good story to tell someday. He made a mental note to tell Pat Weston if he saw her again. She was authorized with a high level of confidentiality clearance. Higher than his own, of that he was sure.

The car went over a couple of extra high bumps and came to a stop. The trunk lid opened and the engine was turned off. Ed climbed out of the trunk. The car was in a double-car garage. The garage door closed and locked into position with a thud. The 'person' door to the Embassy opened and the three of them entered taking their bags and the briefcase with them. They entered a small holding room. The room was empty. On the opposite door from the door they had entered was a second door. It was metal and looked solid. Jack Williams entered a code on a panel and the metal door locked opened with a deep clanging noise. Ed and Mr. Cooper followed Jack Williams into the Embassy. He led them into another room, this time with armed guards as a welcome. Their luggage and the briefcase were X-rayed, and they individually searched.

"You have a gun in this bag," one of the guards stated, pointing at Ed's bag. "Whose bag is it, please?"

"Mine," Ed replied quickly. It hadn't been in his mind to mention it before.

"And?" the guard asked.

Mr. Cooper interrupted. "He's authorized," he said, showing the guard a pass from his wallet.

The guard nodded, motioned for them to move on, and opened the next door. This door took them into the kitchen of the Embassy.

"That reminds me," Mr. Cooper said, taking in the aromas from the smell of food, "we haven't eaten for hours."

"I'll arrange for a bit of a cook-up," Williams said. "I'll see if we've got a spot o' haggis!"

"Let us pray," Mr. Cooper replied, cringing at the thought.

Williams led them through the Embassy to the ambassador's office. The building was old but a wonderful example of classic architecture. The ceilings were twenty or more feet high and the walls held large paintings that showed the magnificence of the building.

"Not a bad place to work," Ed commented as they followed Williams.

"Yesterday, you could say that," Williams said. "But not today!" He knocked on the ambassador's door and entered before waiting for a reply.

Williams introduced Ambassador Sir Jonathon Isaac. He was tall with a full head of red hair. Dressed in a tuxedo, he looked every part the British diplomat. He motioned Ed and Mr. Cooper to take a seat on the sofas away from his desk, and joined them. Williams excused himself and left to arrange for food.

"You catch us at a terrible time," the ambassador said. "Everyone at the Embassy is, and I have to be honest here, extremely worried about Miss Andrews." He shook his head as he spoke.

Ed gulped at the comment, and wanted to speak. He looked to Mr. Cooper instead.

"We understand your concern, of course, Mr. Ambassador," Mr. Cooper said calmly. "But are there particular reasons why your concern is so great? We have little knowledge of Bulgaria and its current issues, perhaps a quick overview would help put us in the picture."

Sir Isaac nodded, undid his bow tie, and sat back into the sofa. "First let me explain the get-up," he said, referring to his tuxedo. "I have an invitation to an opera this evening, and as much as possible we are trying to maintain the norm. It is being held only five minutes from here at the National Theatre, so I have plenty of time to be of assistance to you before I leave. If indeed I do attend. I am in no mood for opera."

"We understand," Mr. Cooper said. "Tell us what we need to know and then let's see where it leaves us."

"First let me give you a thumb-nail sketch of Bulgaria," Ambassador Isaac said. "It will help put today's problem into perspective. The country is, of course, part of the Soviet bloc. That alone makes for uneasy times. The U.S.S.R. is faltering both politically and financially. The old guard is changing and changing often. Those changes affect the entire bloc. In Bulgaria's situation the leader of the Communist party, and therefore the leader of the country is Todor Zhivkov. He has been in power for thirty years. He is certainly a 'strongman', but nowhere near as brutal as other national Communist leaders. People don't fear for their lives in Bulgaria, but they do what they are told to do. Food is on the table and there is fuel in the winters. Education is good and it's free. Stringent compared to our standards, but after thirty years I suspect you get used to it."

"Doesn't sound too bad," Ed offered.

"Up until now," the ambassador agreed, "it hasn't been too bad. But, and there's always a 'but'. Things began to change this year." He chewed on his lip and shook his head. "The country is made up of many ethnic groups, and for the most part they get along. They stick to their own religions and enjoy their own cultures. Things have worked out. However, changes are under way and the hugely significant change affects the mostly Muslim Turkish ethnic group." He looked at Ed. "An arena you have some knowledge of I understand?"

"Extremely limited, Mr. Ambassador," Ed assured him.

"Some is better than none," Mr. Cooper commented.

The ambassador continued. "What happened this year, and is happening as we speak, came out of the blue. President Zhivkov has decreed that all ethnic Turks must exchange their surname from a Turkish name to a Bulgarian name."

"Rather dramatic, no doubt," Mr. Cooper said. "Is there a specific reason that we know of?"

"Our assumption," the ambassador continued, "is that Zhivkov can see changes coming and wants the country to be totally Bulgarian, as it were, before any changes occur. Politically it's a smart move for the majority of Bulgarians who are Bulgarian Orthodox and who see this as an important message to ethnic Turks. It is not a good thing and there have been a number of academia speaking opposed to it."

"But to no avail?" Ed asked.

"None whatsoever. Zhivkov is not going to back down. He has his own problems within the Communist Party. For him to back down would be his end both politically and perhaps literally."

"And how does this relate to our matter at hand?" Mr. Cooper asked.

"Perhaps nothing," the ambassador said, "perhaps everything. The mood of the country has changed since the announcement. Neighbors, who got along just fine before, now take sides strictly along ethnic lines. The 'melting pot' mentality has softened. Gangs are appearing, something unheard of before this year. Now to your specific question, General, we know that many Turks have crossed the border into Turkey. This is relatively easy and cheap for those close to the Turkish border, but considerably more expensive and dangerous for the Turks in, say, Sofia. To get from here to the Turkish border requires money, and lots of it. So our assumption, and it is only an assumption, is that Miss Andrews

has been kidnapped by a group of Turks that need the money to get to
Turkey. And a million dollars will get a lot of people to Turkey. We doubt
this has been organized by a small group of dissatisfied young people.
We're pretty sure it has a large organization behind it."

"That is not good news," Ed said.

"That is bad news," Mr. Cooper elaborated. "We will need to figure
this possibility into our planning."

There was a rap on the door, and Williams stuck his head around
the door. "Dinner is served," he announced looking at Ed and Mr.
Cooper. "And we must get you to the Theatre, Mr. Ambassador. The
car is ready."

Ambassador Isaac left for the opera, promising to be back as quickly
as possible. Ed and Mr. Cooper followed Williams to a room that was
used by the Embassy staff as their lunchroom.

On the table were two plates of steaming hot food. The dish was a
stew like dish with a spicy aroma.

"Excellent," Mr. Cooper said as he sat, not waiting for any formalities.
"And we are eating?" he asked.

"Beef Kavarma Kebap," Williams replied. "I made it myself."

Ed took a taste of the dish. "Hey, this is great. Can I get the recipe?"
Williams smiled.

"I mean it," Ed added, not stopping to eat as he spoke. "We bachelors
have to impress the ladies once in a while."

"My pleasure," Williams said. "I'll get you a copy."

Williams left them to eat.

"So what's our plan?" Ed asked. They were back in the ambassador's
office, refreshed and energized after a good meal.

"Here are my thoughts," Mr. Cooper said, sitting back into the
leather bound chair. "Feel free to challenge any part of it. Whatever we
agree upon, we'll run by the ambassador tonight and make sure he can
support it." He paused, taking a deep breath. "First and foremost the
goal is to get Miss Andrews safely . . ."

Ed nodded. "God yes!"

Mr. Cooper continued. He outlined his plan in as much detail as
he could, given they knew little of what the demands would be as it
related to getting the money to the kidnappers. They discussed the
plan, challenging it at every step. There was no disagreement—just

unanswered and unanswerable, questions. They dealt with the matters of risk as best they could in a cold business-like fashion. An outsider listening in would not have understood that Carolyn was both the daughter of Mr. Cooper's boss and long-time friend, and the person whom Ed so dearly loved.

They reviewed the plan with Ambassador Isaac when he returned from the opera. Mr. Cooper explained the plan; stressing that if the money could be exchanged for Carolyn in a simple swap then all of the planning was not needed.

"Let's hope that's case," the ambassador said thoughtfully. "I'll be happy if we can do the deal and get Miss Andrews back safely. In addition to being a very nice person, she is an excellent worker and has fit in very well here."

"Yes, she has done well," Mr. Cooper mused.

"Do you know she gets by in Bulgarian?" the ambassador asked.

"Sign of a solid Oxford education," Ed said flatly. In his mind he recalled how he often joked about her education being at such a higher level than his.

"Maybe," the ambassador shrugged. "I went to Oxford and I managed through Latin and French; but the Balkan languages—that would have taken a better student than me." The ambassador stood and walked around his office. "Here's what I think gentlemen. It's almost midnight. My place is just a few minutes from here. I'll go home, get a few hours sleep, and be back here by six. I'd suggest you both find the most comfortable spot in the room and settle in. We have no idea what time they will contact us tomorrow, so the sooner we are ready to the better. If the phone rings, answer it. It will be me"

It was agreed. They shook hands with the ambassador and he left for home.

"By the way, Eddie, how's the wound" the General asked.

"Which wound?" Ed replied.

"Good man."

They got as comfortable as they could and tried to sleep. Sleep didn't come easy. Eventually exhaustion took over and they slept.

CHAPTER TWELVE

THURSDAY, OCTOBER 11ᵀᴴ

•••••••

The cleaner entering the ambassador's office woke them. He did not see them on the sofas and plugged in the vacuum cleaner as usual. He jumped as the two heads appeared above the backs of the sofas. He returned their smile and carried on as if he found guests in the ambassador's office regularly. They both sat up and shook their heads. It was five-thirty. If the sun was up, they didn't see it. It was raining lightly. A glum day for their activities, Ed thought. The cleaner, a man in his sixties quickly cleaned the room and left.

The ambassador was on time and Williams who was pushing in a tray of tea and toast followed him into the office. The four of them helped themselves to tea, enjoying the warmth, and comforting taste.

"All three cars are ready to go," Williams said, putting down his cup. "Each of the three drivers is a good man, and will take orders well. They don't know the details of the plan, but are aware of what this is all about. They each know Miss Andrews. We can count on them for sure."

"Excellent. Well done, Williams," the ambassador said. "Let's get the wire on the General and Mr. Crowe. We have to be ready at any moment."

The wire and microphone was attached to Mr. Cooper and the earpiece attached to Ed's ear. They tested it. It worked fine.

"Just keep in mind this only works up to two hundred feet," Williams reminded them. "Beyond that you're out of touch."

95

Together the four went over the plan again. Williams had brought in a map of the city. "Of course it all depends on where they want to meet you, General. It's a big city. Our assumption that it will be in a park makes sense," he shrugged, "but who knows?"

Everyone nodded in agreement. Some assumptions had to be made, and MI6 experience suggested a park. Time would tell.

They sat around the office. Ambassador Isaac moved paper around his desk, accomplishing nothing. Williams and Mr. Cooper shared the previous day's copy of The Telegraph, which was flown in daily from London. Little held their attention. Ed picked up his bag and left the room. He had made a decision, and he didn't want to think about it long enough to change his mind. He entered the toilet area, just as the cleaner was leaving. They exchanged smiles. In the toilet area, he locked the door and dug into his bag. He pulled out his gun, which was still shy two bullets from his shooting in Libya. He attached the holster to his left leg, making sure it was secure and comfortable. He waited several minutes then carried his bag back into the ambassador's office. He crossed his right leg over his left leg, ensuring the gun was not visible. He sat back and waited, not even pretending to read the newspaper. He would have felt guilty if he had done so.

He didn't wait long. At seven-fifteen a guard entered the room with an envelope addressed to Ambassador Isaac.

"Delivered by a young boy," the guard explained. "Couldn't have been more than eight or nine, sir." He saluted and left.

"Here we go gentlemen," the ambassador said, opening the envelope. He read the letter, the strain on his face showing. "Shit," he said rubbing his forehead and giving the letter to Williams. "They want the exchange to take place in fifteen minutes by the fountain in front of the museum."

Williams shook his head. "That's just a five minute walk from here. We can't use the cars. It would be a give-away."

Mr. Cooper gasped in despair. "Now what for God's sake?"

The ambassador stood and walked around his desk. "Let me think," he struggled to speak, "I've got to think."

The others waited. The ambassador came to a decision. "Williams, quickly go find Mr. Eltilib and bring him in here . . . immediately."

Williams ran out of the room.

The ambassador turned to Ed. "Take off your clothes quickly. When Eltilib gets here put on his clothes. You're not a perfect size, but it's the best we can do. General, put the courier's chain on your wrist and attach it to the briefcase. Put the key in your pocket and don't lose it for God's sake!"

Mr. Eltilib, the cleaner, showed a sign of surprise this time. Ed was standing in the middle of the room wearing just his underwear, shoes, and socks. The gun was now visible to everyone. No one commented. Their plan was now useless.

At everyone's encouragement Mr. Eltilib removed his clothes, throwing them to Ed as he did. He reluctantly put on Ed's clothes, walked over to the farthest corner and sat down.

Ambassador Isaac went over his idea in a couple of minutes. It made sense. No one could think of a better plan. It was all they had.

The ambassador opened the map on his desk. "Gentlemen, the fountain is right here," he pointed to the map, "and we are right here! If I took you to the window, I could almost show you where the pick-up point is. These are crafty people gentlemen. Be careful out there."

Ed left the embassy, glad to have Mr. Eltilib's hat to help cover his face and protect him from the rain. He walked slowly and slightly stooped. As he exited the embassy grounds, he turned left—away from the rendezvous point. He didn't look to see if he was being watched; he knew he was. He continued walking for two blocks and turned right. He quickened his pace, but did not run.

Mr. Cooper left minutes later. He walked quickly and stood straight. He wanted to be seen. He wanted to appear confident. He was on his way. He carried the briefcase in his left hand. As he left the embassy grounds, he turned right. Three minutes later he turned left as he reached the National Assembly. The Assembly was a massive triangular-shaped building. The exterior was white, which presented a clean image for the government. The rain was now a drizzle. He turned right at the end of the building, and was now walking along the longer side of the triangle. To his left, halfway up the side of the building was the fountain he was heading toward. The kidnappers had selected wisely. The fountain was in the center of a major traffic intersection. The traffic was light. Better for them, he thought. He kept his head high. He kept his eye on the fountain. From what he could see, there was no one at the fountain. He looked quickly at his watch. The letter had been delivered twenty minutes ago.

Ed was on the other side of the street from Mr. Cooper, half a block back. He kept his head down. He remained stooped. He could see Mr.

Cooper when he glanced his way. He slowed down. He did not want to arrive too closely to Mr. Cooper. There was only going to be one chance. Better late than early, he told himself. He had to fight back the desire to run to the fountain to search for Carolyn. He slowed down even further. He had to clear his mind. He stopped and turned to look at the impressive Archeology Museum in front of him. He had to turn his back on the fountain to admire the Museum. He forced himself to do it. It offered him an opportunity to take a deep breath. He smiled at the Museum, counted to ten and then turned and continued slowly toward the fountain.

Mr. Cooper stood on the curb waiting for the traffic to clear. He was just fifty steps from the fountain. He could see no one at the fountain. As he started to cross the road a taxi pulled up by the fountain and two men got out. The older man walked to the back of the taxi, checking the back lights as if something was wrong. The second, much younger man stood by the back door. He appeared nervous, constantly looking about. When he saw Mr. Cooper crossing the street he spoke to the older man, motioning to Mr. Cooper.

Ed saw Mr. Cooper crossing the street, walking briskly to the fountain—directly toward the taxi. Mr. Cooper stopped ten feet from the taxi and waited.

In his earpiece Ed could hear the other man speak. It was garbled, and meant nothing.

Mr. Cooper's voice was clear. "Where is the girl?" he demanded.

The response was garbled, but it did not matter. What mattered was that he could hear Mr. Cooper. He would take his directions from Mr. Cooper. Nothing else mattered.

"I have the money here in the suitcase; one million US dollars. Give me the girl and I'll give you the money. No girl, no money."

Ed kept walking, judging how far he was from the taxi. Less than one hundred and fifty feet. He slowed again. Looking to his right, away from the taxi.

"No more money," Mr. Cooper said. He spoke loud and clear. He was making a point.

The older man shouted now, and Ed could hear him say the words 'Stonebridge' and seconds later 'MI6'.

Ed now knew they were in trouble. The kidnappers not only knew who Carolyn was, more importantly they knew who her father was and his position at the British Secret Service.

'Take it or leave it," Mr. Cooper said. Ed could see he was holding out the briefcase with his left hand.

Ed sped up, trying not to catch any one's attention. Now less than a hundred feet from the taxi. He reached down and pulled the gun from its holster. He slipped it into his coat pocket, not letting go of it. As he continued forward he clicked off the safety on the gun.

"Put the knife away," Mr. Cooper ordered. "It won't help you. If you don't put it away, I'll leave and you get nothing."

It seemed as if everything went into slow motion. Ed started running toward the taxi. He could hear the man shouting at Mr. Cooper. He looked up as he ran. The younger man was now shouting, shouting in a foreign language to Ed. The older man turned to face Ed, not wanting to take his eyes off Mr. Cooper and the money.

Ed stopped running fifteen feet away from the taxi. He took his left hand out of his coat pocket and raised it in a sign of calm. He looked at the older man, trying to keep calm. He spoke as clearly as he could in Turkish. "Senden cok hoslanıyorum," he said smiling.

The older man turned to Ed with a puzzled look. He turned to the younger man who shrugged his lack of understanding. He turned back to Ed, just as Ed fired his gun that hit him in his left leg. The bullet entered and exited his thigh. Blood poured from both wounds. The man was strong. He grimaced and started moving to Ed with the knife held forward. Ed shot him in his right leg. The man dropped the knife and collapsed, screaming at the top of his voice. Ed turned to the younger man who was now ready to run and moved toward him aiming the gun to his head. He was no more than a boy, and he was terrified.

"Where's the girl?" Ed shouted. No response. "Where's the girl?" he shouted again.

The boy was holding his arms high. He did not want to be shot. He looked at the back seat of the taxi, motioning his head in that direction. Ed walked closer to the car motioning the boy to turn and put his hands on the top of the cab and looked to the rear of it. Mr. Cooper had his foot on the throat of the man on the ground, who was going nowhere.

On the back seat was a blanket covering a body. It did not move. Ed held the gun to the boy and had him widen his stance as he leaned against the car trunk. Stepping back, and regretting it immediately, Ed kicked him from behind smacking him solidly in his groin with full force. The boy collapsed with a terrible groan, holding his groin as he rolled on the ground.

"Oh my God," Mr. Cooper said, pulling a face.

Ed opened the back door of the vehicle, pulling the blanket away from Carolyn. She was lying face up, with her hands tied behind her back and her ankles tied together. She was gagged with a towel tied at the back of her head. Her eyes were full of terror, and recognizing Ed she collapsed into tears.

"It's okay. You're okay," Ed reassured her, untying the gag. "Try not to move."

She took a deep breath as the gag came off. "Try not to move?" she shouted. "How am I supposed to move when I'm tied hand and foot?"

"I'll be back," Ed said, leaving her as she was. He stood back from the vehicle. The boy was recovering, but not about to run away. Mr. Cooper had his foot on the man's throat still, but not as heavily. Mr. Cooper held the knife.

He looked at the vehicle. "Is she there? Is she okay?" Unknowingly, he stepped harder on the throat as he spoke.

Ed called back. "Yes she's here, and I'm pretty sure she's okay. She's told me off already." He went back to untying Carolyn.

In the distance the sound of emergency cars got closer. A crowd was now gathering.

Untied, Carolyn got out of the taxi and took in the surroundings. She was still groggy, but sufficiently aware of herself to straighten up her clothes and, seemingly unconsciously, fix up her hair.

"Thanks, Ed," she said. "You'll never know how glad I was to see you, and how scared I've been these past two days." She leaned against the cab.

Ed thought she was going to faint. And then slowly, she did. Ed broke her fall, catching her gently and safely. He could feel her breathing and her warm body against his. He was still holding her in his arms when the ambulance attendants took her very gently from him.

The boy had been attended to, and was now telling his story to the police. He pointed to Ed several times as he told what happened, or at least his side of it.

Ambulance personnel had stopped the bleeding for the older man, and had bandaged both his legs. As he was carried into the ambulance he was raving and pointing in Ed's direction. Ed didn't care, but walked over to Mr. Cooper who was trying, unsuccessfully, to speak to the police.

The officer with Mr. Cooper turned to Ed, took a quick look at the older man now shouting from inside the ambulance, and put his hand out to Ed—palm up. Knowing what he wanted, Ed took the gun from his pocket and handed it to the officer making sure the safety catch was on. Following instructions, Ed put out both hands and he was handcuffed. Mr. Cooper tried to explain, but it was of no use.

As he was led away, Ed heard Carolyn call out. He recognized her voice, but not the language. The police officer walked over to Carolyn, listening to what she said. He took notes, nodding that he understood. Carolyn was having trouble with some of her translation, and was visibly frustrated. The police officer indicated his understanding, and appeared to be helping her with her words.

As Ed was escorted to the police car, he took the opportunity to lean over to Carolyn, who was now sitting up on the stretcher. He kissed her forehead. "Senden cok hoslanıyorum," he said. "Look after yourself. I'll be back soon."

"They wouldn't listen, Ed," she said. "I tried to explain. I told them you have diplomatic immunity." She shook her head in frustration. "I am so sorry."

Ed was assisted in the back of a police car, which drove away with its lights flashing.

Mr. Cooper joined Carolyn and the paramedics in the ambulance. It drove at high speed, following the ambulance that held the two men and several police officers.

"What's with the Turkish?" Mr. Cooper asked.

"Oh that," Carolyn blushed. "He just told me that he liked me a lot."

"That's interesting," Mr. Cooper said. "You'll be pleased to know that he said the exact same thing to one of your kidnappers."

"Really?"

"Really!" Mr. Cooper replied. "Just before he shot him."

"Ed shot someone?"

"Twice. Just to be sure."

Carolyn tried sitting up, but was held down by a paramedic. "The man in the ambulance? I thought the police had shot him!"

"Not this time. And I won't even tell you what he did to the young boy."

"Please, General, please tell me,' Carolyn pleaded.

Mr. Cooper told her.

"Bloody hell," Carolyn exclaimed. "What has happened to our junior consultant?"

"He's turned into a full fledged operative, that's what I think."

Carolyn thought for a moment. "What about, you know; Libya?"

"Shot him too."

Carolyn gasped. "Killed him?"

"No. Just shot him. I'll explain later."

They held their conversation as the ambulance pulled into the Emergency entrance of the hospital.

The handcuffs were attached to a chain that was itself bolted to the center of the table. He was comfortable. He had been treated well on the drive to the police station. More importantly Carolyn was safe, and as best he could tell no real harm had happened to her. He smiled at the gutsy way she had reacted after he had released the gag from her mouth. Tough lady, he said to himself.

The door opened and two men entered the room. One stood by the door. The second man sat across from Ed and opened a file he had placed on the table.

"Mr. Crowe I believe?"

"Yes, sir."

"Both a British and Canadian subject?"

"Yes sir."

"And the lady told my officers you are part of the British Embassy staff, but you have not been registered as such. Is that correct?"

"Yes, sir."

"You will excuse me," he said, looking at Ed's clothing, "you do not look like a British diplomat."

"No, sir."

"You look more to me like a tramp, no?"

"They are not my clothes, sir."

The man looked down at the file.

"You shot a Bulgarian citizen and seriously damaged another. Are these the regular actions of a British diplomat?"

Ed took a breath. "No, sir, of course not. But I was protecting myself and other members of the British Embassy."

"And what are your exact duties with the British Embassy, Mr. Crowe?"

Ed thought about that, maintaining eye contact. "I think I need to see a representative from the Embassy please," he replied.

The man shrugged. "Such a simple question, Mr. Crowe."

Ed smiled, and took a chance. "Under section 71 of the United Nations Treaty on . . . ," but he was interrupted.

The man held up his hand, frustrated. "Enough, enough. How can police do their job with such obstacles? You will spend the night in our cells, and I will arrange for such a visit. Only it will be on my terms, Mr. Crowe." He stood, walked to the door, and turned. "On my terms, Mr. Crowe."

"I also have orders to follow, sir," Ed said, hoping to repair their now cold relationship.

The men left the room.

The cell turned out to be like every cell he had seen on television. It was no more than eight feet by ten feet. It held a bed, a chair, a toilet, and a sink. The light, for what it was worth, shone from a fluorescent fixture built into the ceiling. There was no window, no books, not even a Bible to turn to. The two meals he received were served on paper plates. The food was edible, but not much more so than the plates themselves. No one visited. No one spoke. It gave him time to think. He thought about bird watching and the many new birds he had listed since moving to Canada. He made a mental list of the next ten birds he would look for next spring.

The light went out some hours later, and he stumbled to his bed. He was exhausted and fell asleep in minutes.

CHAPTER THIRTEEN

FRIDAY, OCTOBER 12ᵀᴴ

• • • ● ● ● • •

Carolyn woke quickly, and had to remind herself where she was. The medical staff in the emergency ward had examined her with great care and attention. She was de-hydrated, physically exhausted, and showed mild signs of depression. She argued that her intermittent crying was normal given what she had been through and argued strongly against the doctor adding depression to the official list of conditions. The doctor conceded. He was not accustomed to patients arguing his diagnoses, and if complying with Carolyn made her feel better about herself, he was happy to so oblige.

Carolyn cleaned up; dressing in the most business-like suit she carried in her bag that had been safely retrieved from the trunk of the kidnappers' taxi. She wanted, indeed needed, to feel back to normal; as back to normal as the recent events would allow. When Mr. Cooper knocked on her door, she was ready to go. She gave him a hug and thanked him for his help in bringing her back to safety. He tried unsuccessfully to hide his embarrassment. She tried to pretend she did not notice it.

"So where is Ed, General?" she asked, picking up her bag.

"He's still being held at the police station. Our plan is to have him released today."

Her manner turned serious. "General, he should not have been held this long. We must get him released now, this morning."

"We must leave it to the Ambassador, Miss Andrews. All is in hand. For now, I am to get you to the airport. A plane will be waiting to fly you to England immediately and I will be joining you."

"That is not acceptable, General," she stated. "I will not leave until I know Ed is safely at the Embassy." She paused. "He saved my life. I cannot leave him in custody while I fly home to bloody England." Her voice was raised.

"Miss Andrews, please don't make me repeat my orders. I care for Eddie, as much as I care for anyone. My orders, our orders, are to go back to England—today. We can address our concerns to our superiors when we get home . . ."

"That's my father for God's sake. Let me phone him now. You don't understand, General . . ." the bag slipped from her hand, and she put both hands to her mouth to control her emotions. "Ed and I are . . . we're . . . we're friends, General, very good friends. I can't just . . . Oh God, and I sent him that letter . . ."

"We must leave now," he said, picking up her bag. "Trust the process, Miss Andrews—Carolyn. Please trust the process."

He opened the door for her and they left for the airport.

When they were safely in the air, Mr. Cooper explained the events that were driving the process and keeping Ed at the police station.

Ed woke with the light going on after a good night's sleep. The bed was not comfortable, but he had been exhausted enough to not to notice it. His watch had been taken from him, so he was not aware of the time. He was refreshed and ready to face the day.

Breakfast was delivered through the mail-drop feature of the door with no words offered from the unseen guard. After finishing it completely and quickly, he sat back on the bed and waited.

He did not have long to wait. A guard entered the cell and escorted Ed back to the same interview room he was in the day before. He was handcuffed and shackled to the table again. The guard stood by the door, and the interviewer from yesterday joined them. He placed the same file on the table. He was, Ed could see, still not in a friendly mood.

"Will my representative from the Embassy be joining us soon?" Ed asked.

"They have declined to join us today, Mr. Crowe. You must look after yourself it would appear."

Ed closed his eyes to think. There was something wrong, terribly wrong. The Embassy not sending someone made no sense. The message from Ambassador Isaac reflected a positive relationship between the UK and Bulgarian governments. Neither Carolyn nor Mr. Cooper would leave him unprotected. Something was wrong and he had to think it through.

"So you are a member of MI6. Mr. Crowe?" the man asked directly

"No, I am not."

The man shrugged. "This could take all day or we can get to the point quickly, Mr. Crowe. We do not appreciate foreign spies working in our country."

"My name is Edwin William Crowe, and I am both a British and Canadian subject. If you want to arrest me, please do so and I will then ask to be represented by counsel."

The man laughed. "Spies who shoot people do not get access to counsel in Bulgaria, Mr. Crowe, they go to prison. It is not a nice prison, and you do not get three meals a day. Now be honest with me, and I'll see you are looked after well."

Ed shook his head, trying to smile. He could not understand what was going on. Why had he been left to look after himself? His head was spinning. "Please phone the British Embassy for me," he asked.

The man motioned with his hands. "I phoned them myself this morning, Mr. Crowe. They deny knowing who you are and why you shot the taxi driver and abused the young man."

"Could I get a cup of tea?" Ed asked.

After an exchange in words, the guard left the room.

"Tea is not the answer, Mr. Crowe. Simply answering my questions will resolve everything, and have you back to your friends and family in Oakville."

Ed nodded and smiled. If the interviewer had been more observant, he would have noticed Ed's hands relax and would not have taken Ed's smile as a smirk.

The guard re-entered with a large cup of tea and placed it in front of Ed. Taking a long sip of tea, Ed thought for a moment. "Perhaps you are correct, sir. If my people are not here to help me, then I must help myself."

The man nodded, opened the file again, and selected a pen to take notes.

"A wise choice, Mr. Crowe, a wise choice indeed. Now let us begin with some basics."

Ed nodded taking another sip of tea.

"You live in Oakville, Canada?"

"Yes."

"You are a member of MI6?"

"Sometimes."

"You have recently done work for them?"

"Yes."

"And you were paid of course?"

"Of course."

"Where would that have been?"

"Turkey."

"Your friend Mr. Cooper. He is a member of MI6?"

"Yes."

"He recruited you?"

"Yes."

"Now you came to Bulgaria to assist in the safe return of, Miss Andrews?"

"Yes."

"And you shot a man in doing so?"

"Yes."

"Do you have any regrets in shooting this man?"

"No."

"Even though the Embassy is not here to help you?"

"That, of course, I find disturbing. But I am glad I helped in the release."

The questions continued for half an hour before they took a break for food. The questions continued after the break.

"You know who the chief of the British Intelligence Service is?"

"It is Lord Stonebridge," Ed spoke coldly.

"One final question Mr. Crowe. What do you think of Lord Stonebridge?"

Ed thought for a moment. "I think he is a bit of a tight-ass who doesn't fully appreciate the work his daughter does."

The man looked up from his note taking, taken aback with the response. "Really?" he said. "That is interesting."

Closing the file, he left the room. He returned twenty minutes later.

"I have spoken with your Embassy, Mr. Crowe. They want you delivered to their private plane at the airport in an hour. You are to be flown back to England today."

"What about my clothes?" Ed asked.

The man shrugged. "What can I say? I cannot speak to their actions."

The plane ride was comfortable, although the crew made comments about Ed's clothes and unshaven face.

"It's what you must do for your country," Ed commented.

As usual, he made coffee and delivered cups to the pilot and co-pilot.

"Was your operation a success in Bulgaria?" the pilot asked, being sure not to delve too deeply into its purpose.

"We'll see when we arrive in England," Ed said tentatively. "It may be a different reception than normal." He didn't expand, and the pilot didn't ask further.

"Are you aware of what happened today in England?" the pilot asked.

Ed shook his head. "No. No one's told me anything."

"There's been a bomb in Brighton, at the Conservative Party's convention. It was aimed at Mrs. Thatcher. Last we heard five people were killed. Mr. Thatcher and her husband are okay."

"Oh my God," Ed exclaimed. "Any idea who's responsible?"

"Who would you guess?" the pilot asked, knowing the answer was obvious.

Ed went back to his seat for the remainder of the flight.

The regular driver met him at the plane's arrival at the airfield. It was raining heavily. It was October, after all, Ed thought, rushing to get into the car. Ed recognized the drive to the Inn. He did not expect to be driven to Stonebridge Manor this time. Things had changed. He would soon find out how much things had changed.

He thanked the driver and entered the Inn. The manager recognized him and pointed him into the restaurant to the left of the reception desk. At the far end of the room Lord Stonebridge sat alone at a table for eight. It was clear of cutlery and tablecloth. Keeping his head up and his back straight, Ed walked quietly through the carpeted restaurant. He stood in front of the table.

"Good evening, Lord Stonebridge." he said with a smile. "It's good to see you again."

"Have a seat, Mr. Crowe," Lord Stonebridge replied, not standing or offering his hand. "You're aware, no doubt, of the circumstances in Brighton?"

"Yes, sir. Just the basics."

"The police are still working on it. We'll be involved soon no doubt." He shuffled some papers on the table, making the point he was reading from them.

Lord Stonebridge looked up, rolling his eyes. "So you think I'm a bit of a tight-ass, if you'll excuse my English, who doesn't appreciate his daughter?"

"That's what I said, sir."

Lord Stonebridge banged the table with both hands and laughed loudly. He stood and offered his hand. "Welcome back, Mr. Crowe, you did a wonderful job. A bloody wonderful job indeed."

"Thank you, sir," Ed responded, pulling up a chair.

"So tell me," Lord Stonebridge asked, "When did you catch on?"

"This morning. I couldn't figure it out for a while, and then I recalled they knew I was both Canadian and British and that made no sense. And this morning he knew I lived in Oakville. Well the only way that was possible was if you told him, or someone told him."

"Brilliant. Well done. And I see you didn't give them any information that was in any way protected."

"I'm not really sure I know anything protected. Besides their questions were limited to what you wanted to ask, so I assumed you wouldn't ask anything of real importance; just in case."

"Just in case you did 'turn on us', to spite the fact that we did not support you in you time of need?"

"Yes, sir."

"And what's you opinion now Mr. Crowe?"

"About the fact that you tested me?"

"Under very difficult circumstances, yes."

Ed shrugged. "I have to be honest with you, Lord Stonebridge. Part of the reason I did not let my mind get the better of me, was my knowledge that your daughter was okay. I think highly of your daughter, and if she had not have been safe I think I would have cracked."

"Fully understandable, Mr. Crowe, as would have I. I should say that it wasn't planned to test you, but when the police took you away it did seem like a fine opportunity." Lord Stonebridge moved his chair in closer to the table, and motioned Ed to do the same. He spoke quietly. "It won't surprise you that most conversations in this building are recorded. We refer to them as 'the Nixon' tapes. What I want to say to you personally is to thank you most deeply, on behalf of both myself and my wife, for returning Carolyn to us. The General has explained the course of events and he has no doubt, as do I, that things would not be as they are without your courage and strength of character. Thank you again." He stood and shook Ed's hand. "Now let's get the General in here and eat." He waved toward the front of the room, and within seconds the room was abuzz with serving staff.

Mr. Cooper marched down between the tables and chairs, his arms out and a big smile on his face. "Well done, Eddie, my boy. I knew you'd prove me right, even under those difficult circumstances." He hugged Ed briefly, which for him was an extreme show of emotion.

The three of them sat at a table and were quickly served with soup and a variety of sandwiches. They didn't speak for a while but enjoyed each other's company silently. Ed hadn't eaten a real meal in several days, and Lord Stonebridge and Mr. Cooper had delayed eating until Ed had arrived. They wanted to enjoy in the success. The faxed copy of the questions and answers put to Ed in Sofia had been relayed to them prior to Ed leaving the police station. Worried at first, they felt more comfortable as they read further. It was a give-away with Ed's final answer.

"I should tell you, Mr. Crowe," Lord Stonebridge said, "that this was not just a test on you. It is what we call the One Time Test, or OTT, in the department. It happens to all operatives, but it is strictly a non discussable issue. There are two reasons for the test. First to see how the operatives handle themselves, and you did fine. But just as important, it is called One Time, because it only happens one time. Any future stress situations you may find yourself in will be real. Understood?"

"Fully, sir. And thank you for telling me,"

Ed picked up the small cup of tea, and appropriately extended his little finger. He smiled, remembering that Carolyn had jokingly chided him for doing so. He looked to his left. Through the window he could see the table where they had been sitting at the time.

"Could I ask how Carolyn is?" Ed asked cheerfully.

Both started to reply, but Mr. Cooper took the lead. "Let me answer that, sir," he said looking at Lord Stonebridge. He turned to Ed. "Carolyn is doing very well, probably as well as can be expected. She is currently undergoing tests at our special ward in London," he smiled, "and we expect she will be out and about by tomorrow. Lady Stonebridge has asked that Carolyn not be disturbed, and she did say you would understand."

"Of course, yes I certainly do understand. Thank you." Ed was relieved.

Lord Stonebridge coughed. "What the General is not telling you, Mr. Crowe, is that my daughter was insistent that you be released before she left Bulgaria. I think the expression 'insubordination' came close to the front."

Ed smiled widely. "Thank you, Lord Stonebridge; I appreciate both your candor and Carolyn's concern."

They turned back to their tea and 'afters' as Mr. Cooper referred to them. Ed was tempted to use the Canadian 'dessert', but did not. The thought, however, did remind him that he had to go home.

"When do I return to Canada?" Ed asked smiling, with his small finger fully extended.

"As soon as we get you cleaned up, back in your own clothes and ready," Mr. Cooper said, holding his cup of tea with his hand wrapped around it, not letting the handle get in the way. "Your clothes and luggage are here, so when you're ready to start?"

"Let's go," Ed said.

Lord Stonebridge excused himself after thanking Ed again, promising to pass on Ed's best wishes to Carolyn and Lady Stonebridge.

Changing in the room Ed noticed the envelope in the inside pocket of his jacket. Carolyn's letter. He decided he would re-read it on the plane back to Canada; on the flight home.

Mr. Cooper drove with him to the airport. It was still raining, but had turned into a drizzle.

"I understand Paris is nice at this time of year," Mr. Cooper said, looking out into the rain.

"Sorry," Ed didn't follow the change of subjects.

"That's her next assignment. Or so I understand. Nice place Paris."

"Probably a lot safer than Turkey or Bulgaria," Ed added.

"Probably."

"Thanks for the heads-up. Probably no need for any of my in-depth international experience in Paris."

"Probably not."

They drove on in silence, not speaking until the car drove into the airport and onto the runway.

"You did very well, Eddie. Don't let your passport expire."

"I'll keep that in mind Mr. Cooper. Thanks for your faith in me."

"Well proven as it turns out."

They shook hands. Ed got out of the car, collected his luggage, and entered the plane that was waiting for him. He waved into the cockpit, told them he would be making coffee in twenty minutes, and took his seat. Knowing it was a long flight back to Toronto, he decided to take Pat's advice and write out a full report on his activities. It would help him get matters into perspective, and as Pat had convinced him, 'writing it down' helped put it behind him; it became history.

The plane took off and within minutes they were above the clouds. The sky was now blue and clear, the clouds below and behind them. He felt better, much better. He looked at his watch. By the time they landed and he grabbed a taxi, he would still have time to make it to The Queen's Head. He would be late for his Friday beer, but he'd be home. No more guns, no more danger.

He made the coffee and took two cups to the cockpit. The sky was more visible through the forward window and he lingered for a few minutes to take in the view. Returning to the table at the rear of the plane he collected paper for his report and the envelope from his jacket. He set the paper aside took a sip of his coffee and picked up the envelope. Something was strange. It was thinner than he had expected. He withdrew the paper and opened it. It was a recipe for 'Beef Kavarma Kebap' with an 'As requested' notation from Jack Williams scribbled on it. He chuckled put it aside, and started working on his report.

As he was accustomed to, he wrote in detail what had happened in both Libya and Bulgaria. He worded it carefully, remembering Pat's advice—or was it a direction—not to identify anyone by name. Those who would be reading the report with the appropriate approval would know who the players were. Adding names only added risks. He stopped working on the report several times, wondering where the letter from Carolyn was. He couldn't think of any specific risk in the letter being circulated. In the end he realized he was over-reacting to any 'risk'. It was a 'Dear John" letter, no more and no less. He dropped the issue from his head and went back to writing his report and making coffee for himself and the cockpit crew.

It was dark outside as the plane descended and he took his regular seat and buckled in. His report was complete. He had moved it into history.

The plane landed and taxied to a hanger away from the main terminal. He thanked the pilot and co-pilot, grabbed his bag and saw the limousine pull up ten feet away. Looking around, he did not recognize where he was. He turned back to the plane and called out. "Is this Toronto or Hamilton, guys?"

The answer came from behind him. "It's Ottawa. Don't you recognize your own Capital?" It was Pat's voice.

He turned, caught off guard. Pat was in rear of the limousine speaking through the window. "Come on, get in," she said. "It's cold out there."

He threw his bag into the limousine and followed it in. "What am I doing here? I thought . . ." He shrugged. "I guess I don't know what I thought. Anyway," he said, leaning over and giving her a hug, "it's sure nice to see a friendly face."

She responded with a quick but short hug. "Well, Mr. Crowe, you've got a choice. You can have the driver drop me off at my apartment and have him continue on a five hour drive to Oakville, or—and it's entirely your choice—you can accept my offer to be my guest for the night and we can sort out getting you home tomorrow."

He smiled, not giving it a thought. "I accept your most generous offer without exception Miss, er Miss . . ."

"Weston, smart ass."

"Without exception Miss Weston. I look forward to a most enjoyable Friday night in the Capital."

She leaned over, spoke to the driver, and then turned to Ed. "And don't get any funny ideas. This is all business."

"Why nothing else crossed my mind, Miss Weston."

"Okay, give it up, Ed."

He took her hand and held it for just a second. "It really is good to see you, Pat. I really am pleasantly surprised to see you. Have you eaten?"

"No. Have you?"

"No. But I've got a great recipe in my pocket for an occasion such as this." He patted his jacket.

"You're full of it, ya' know, Ed, you're really full of it. But it is nice to see you again. Maybe you can bring me up-to-date on all of your doings?"

He took the report from his jacket, and showed her. "It's all here, Pat, all here. It's as if the Gods knew we were going to meet tonight."

"You are so totally full of it."

"Not so quick," he said pulling out the recipe. "Do you have a niece piece of beef, an onion, garlic, corn flour, beef stock, paprika, salt, and pepper?"

"No problem there."

"Ah, there's one more ingredient." He chewed his bottom lip, thinking.

"Well, what is it for God's sake?" She was laughing now.

"Hmm, this is unusual." He hummed and asked seriously. "Do you have—a glass of wine?"

She tilted her head. "Well isn't that just the strangest thing? On the assumption you would accept my invitation; I did go out of my way to pick up some wine. Several bottles actually."

"Ha, ha," he said rubbing his hands. "Then I shall be the executive chef, and you the executive sommelier."

"Sounds like a plan. Now let me point out some of downtown Ottawa to you. I've asked the driver to take us on a bit of a tour."

Pat pointed out the regular tourist attractions. The House of Commons with The Peace Tower, the Supreme Court building, the hotel Chateau Laurier, the Sparks Street pedestrian mall, and many more locations that Ed knew by name only. As Ed expected, she was very knowledgeable on her facts and history. When the tour was complete they drove to her apartment, only minutes away from the hub of Ottawa.

As they entered the apartment Pat's cat, Robin, rushed to the door for attention. Pat picked him up and gave him a good rub and scratch. He purred immediately.

"He enjoys his Friday night too," she said, putting him down and topping up his food.

Ed looked around and walked to the balcony door. "Nice apartment, nice view."

"Thanks," Pat said, joining him. "Usual rules. If you recall them?"

"Your room is yours. My room is mine. You're first in the bathroom in the morning. And you're the boss. Correct?"

"Close enough," she smiled. "And the other rule, the department rule?"

"That you cannot have any form of relationship with members of your own department or other similar national departments."

"Correct. And, Ed, for sure you're MI6 now. I don't want to be a pain in the you-know-where, but it's only fair we understand. Okay?"

"That we can't sleep together. I understand, Pat." He leaned over and kissed her on her forehead. "Just don't try it on me okay?"

She smiled, and steered him to his room. "I'll do my best to keep my hands off you."

Twenty minutes later they were relaxing and enjoying each other's company. Ed was cutting up the ingredients as outlined in the recipe. Pat had poured them a glass of wine each and began reading Ed's report. Robin was washing himself on the chesterfield.

Pat read the report, commenting briefly as she read certain passages. "Good, very good."

"Interesting . . ."

"Good team-work. Well done." She kept reading, and suddenly looked up at Ed. "You had to take a piss?" she asked, now speaking louder and laughing.

"I think I referred to it as urinating; if my memory serves me correctly," he replied, putting down a knife and picking up his wine.

"You call it what you like. A piss is a piss."

"Let's meet half way and refer to the event as a pee, okay?"

"Sure, let's do that, Ed." She paused. "You had to take a pee?"

He didn't respond. She read on.

"Jesus, you did shoot him?" Pat asked looking up with a frown.

"Did you suspect I'd shot him?"

Pat put the report down. "I didn't tell you, but Carolyn phoned me a few days ago saying you were in hospital, and they had a photo of the man you were after. But it showed he'd been hanged."

Ed nodded. "Read on."

"Actually she said she'd phone me with an update and she never did. I heard through official channels you were on your way back."

"Read on," Ed said, taking a drink of his wine.

Pat continued reading, pulling faces several times. "Oh my God," Pat exclaimed. "Shot, committed suicide, and hanged for good luck. What kind of a world were you dealing with?"

"It gets more interesting," Ed said, cutting up the beef in thin strips. "You're making it sound worse than it seemed at the time. Keep reading."

Pat read on, keeping her wine in her hand. She sipped on it regularly.

"Not again for crying out loud," Pat gasped. "You're officially dead again? Keep going like this and you'll turn into a cat." She topped up their glasses.

Ed continued cooking, waited for what he thought would be her biggest surprise. It didn't take long.

"Oh no!" she exclaimed, "Not Carolyn. They kidnapped Carolyn? I don't believe this."

Ed tried to respond, but she interrupted. "Of course I believe it, but . . . but . . ."

Ed walked over to the table where Pat sat. "Look I should have warned you. I wasn't sure how much you knew. But please read the report to the end. It all turned out fine in the end."

Pat put her head down and didn't comment or look up until she had finished reading his report. When she was finished, she pushed it away from herself as if doing so would soften its contents.

"So you shot a man in Libya, shot another one in Bulgaria—twice— and then kicked a young boy in the . . ."

"Groin," Ed said, quickly interrupting.

"And then kicked a young boy in the groin?" Pat finished her question.

Ed sat at the table, and rubbed his head. "You know when you say it like that it sounds pretty awful, doesn't it? It all seemed to happen so quickly at the time. Perhaps I'm not cut out for this after all?"

Pat waved his comment off. "Oh don't be so dramatic. Of course you're cut out for this. Your report proves that. Just get back to cooking will you? It's getting late." She pointed him to the kitchen.

He went back to cooking. He appreciated her comments, but kept his thoughts to himself.

"Besides, the alternative of kicking him in the groin area," she said, emphasizing the word 'groin', "was to shoot him. That would have been a bit extreme." She paused. "Anyway, you only had two bullets left, right?"

Ed looked at her in awe.

She shrugged his look off. "Well you did, didn't you?"

He nodded his agreement. "If you put it like that, yes."

"As you said everything's turned out just fine," Pat said, topping up their glasses. "Carolyn's back in England; one bad guy is dead; another bad guy is regretting he kidnapped a young lady; and a young man has learned a good lesson. Let's eat."

"You do have a way of summing things up!" Ed started serving the meal.

The meal, they agreed, was very good. Pat copied the recipe. After cleaning up the mess Ed had made, they wandered out onto the balcony.

"Pretty nippy," Ed remarked.

"A true gentleman would put his arm around his hostess to keep here comfortable," Pat shivered.

He moved closer and put his arm around her. She snuggled up to him.

"As they would say across the river, 'merci'," Pat said, snuggling in as close as she could.

"Quebec?"

"Oui."

"It feels nice to hold you like this," Ed said, keeping his attention on the view across the river.

"Did you ever take French in school?" Pat asked, ignoring his comment.

"No, there were never enough French teachers. Your body feels wonderfully warm."

"Do you need to do a wash before you leave?"

"Do you mean underwear and stuff?" he asked laughing.

"Well you did the last time you visited me."

"No, I have just enough to get me back tomorrow. But thanks for asking."

"Ah, well there's a bit of an issue there."

He looked down at her. She had a sheepish look. "I'm afraid I told your boss that you wouldn't be in until Tuesday. I kinda thought you might want to spend a day or two here with me in Ottawa."

"Really?"

"Was that being too pushy? You don't have to stay . . . with the rules and all!"

He chuckled. "I'd love to stay an extra day or two with you Pat. Rules and all."

"Then maybe we should call it a night and make it an early up and out in the morning?"

"Terrific, I'll do your wash first thing." She moved to leave.

"Can I kiss you good night Pat?"

"No."

"Just here on the balcony."

"No."

"I won't put my hands up your top, honest."

"No, I don't believe you."

"I just want to thank my hostess for a wonderful evening."

She took a deep breath. "Just a little one then."

He took her in his arms and gently kissed her. She moved into his body, and he kissed her more firmly. As he did, he slipped his hands up the back of her blouse and spread his hands across her back. She reacted to the coldness of his hands by moving even closer to him and giggling.

"I knew you would do that," she looked up and slowly pushed him away.

"I knew you'd know that. You're a smart lady."

She smiled, shaking her head. "Let's go in and call it a night."

They finished cleaning up the kitchen, fed Robin, and went to their separate bedrooms.

CHAPTER FOURTEEN

SATURDAY, OCTOBER 13TH

• • • • • • •

He saw the bullet from Gaddafi's gun move ever so slowly toward him. He wanted to get out of its way, but he couldn't move. His feet were fixed to the ground. The bullet hit and he screamed. He felt it enter him, ripping the skin, slowly move through his body and exiting with a larger rip of his skin. He screamed again. He was shaking now uncontrollably. His body was soaking wet.

"Ed, Ed, wake up." Pat was shaking him, holding him by both arms. "You're having a dream. Wake up!" She was shouting now.

He woke with a start. Her face only inches from his, calling his name. He shook his head; he had to clear his mind. She stopped shaking him, and let go of his arms.

"Ed, you're okay. You had a bad dream." She tried to smile, to calm him down.

He sat half up, leaning against the headboard of the bed. He was groggy, but awake. "Sorry. Jesus what a nightmare!" He looked down at his drenched body. "I need a drink of water," he spluttered.

"You stay here, I'll get it." She walked to the door, and turned. "Remember, I know you sleep in the nude."

She returned with a glass of water and a small towel. He drank the water in a gulp, and wiped down his chest to dry off.

"You're sweating like a pig," Pat said looking down at him.

He took a long gulp of air and swallowed. "My mother told me that horses sweat, men perspire, and women dew."

She nodded. "Fair enough, but next time you speak to you mother tell her there's a new category; and that MI6 spies sweat like pigs."

"Okay, I'll tell her." He pulled the sheet up to cover himself fully. "Sorry about that. I feel like a fool."

She offered him new bedding, but he declined.

"Okay, go back to sleep," she told him. "And when you come out in the morning, with some clothes on, bring the bedding with you, I'll add it to the laundry."

She left the room, switching off the light as she did. Her motherly instincts surprised her. She fell asleep, trying to convince herself that the fragrance of his sweat wasn't really rather attractive.

He woke to the sound of the washing machine running at the other end of the apartment. It was mildly comforting. The bang on the door wasn't.

"Okay sleepy head, let's go. Time to get up," Pat called at the door. "And don't forget those stinky sheets."

Such a politician he thought. He threw on some pants, stripped the bed, and took the whole mess across the length of the apartment. He placed it gently on the floor, next to his dirty shirts.

"Do you have underwear on?" Pat enquired.

"Not yet. I'm just about to jump in the shower. No sense getting them dirty for five minutes of wear, is it?"

She wrinkled her nose at the thought. Her motherly deposition was quickly dissipating. "Uggh!" was all she could muster.

Ten minutes later he was showered, shaved, and fully dressed. "How do I look?" he asked, twirling like a model.

"A hell of a lot better than you did at three-thirty this morning," she offered, throwing a pile of clothes in the dryer. "And don't peek over here. I'm washing my own stuff first."

He poured himself a cup of tea and walked onto the balcony. The day was sunny and bright, but cold. He took in the view, impressed at how much was clustered in the central area of Ottawa. It was a nice city he thought, and probably a nice place to live.

"Do you prefer this to Oakville?" he asked, walking back into the apartment.

She looked up from separating clothes. "You know sometimes are better than others for asking questions like that! When one's head is stuck in a mess of dirty male underwear, neither place appears exactly exotic do they?"

"Can I help?" he offered.

"Don't even come close Mr. Crowe, or you'll end up doing this all by yourself." She lifted a pair of his underpants. "Is this blood?"

"Yeah," he said, wishing now he had thrown them away, "but it's *my* blood."

She stood up straight, holding them toward him.

"Right," he said, "out they go." He took them from her with two fingers. "What should I do with them?"

She looked at him, closed her eyes, and prayed.

"Okay, okay, I'll throw them down the garbage chute in the hallway." He started to leave.

"Just make sure none of my neighbors see you carrying that piece of whatever-it-is, mister. I have a reputation to live up to."

He left the apartment with a cheeky smile on his face. He twirled the underwear on his middle finger, hoping a neighbor would see its departure. No one did.

"When we're done here, can I buy you breakfast?" he asked returning to the apartment.

"When *we're* done?"

He raised his hand in agreement. "Let me re-phrase that. When you are done here, would you be good enough to let me buy you breakfast . . . brunch even?"

"That would be lovely, Ed," she said mumbling, "if I still have an appetite for food that is." She picked up another pile for the washer.

They walked to the Sparks Street pedestrian mall. Both were hungry, but ate lightly after Pat had offered to make a fancy meal for supper. They strolled downtown Ottawa. Pat provided a great deal of history. Ed was particularly interested in the history of the Rideau Canal that connected the Ottawa River to Lake Ontario at Kingston.

"So I could go back to Oakville by boat?" he asked.

"You could, and in the summer many people do," Pat answered.

They were by the canal, looking down at one of the locks. "And before you ask," she added, "there are forty-seven locks and it's one-hundred and twenty-five miles long."

"And all that work just for protection from America?"

"Keep in mind," Pat said, as they continued walking, "Kingston was the first capital of Canada. It was moved to Ottawa to make the capital a safer place; and ultimately the canal was built."

"Amazing. And all I learned in school about Canada was the Hudson Bay Company, the fur traders, and the CPR."

They walked for four more hours, enjoyed several cups of Tim Horton's coffee—to which Ed now assumed he was close to addicted—and returned to Pat's apartment exhausted. They made a pot of tea and took their steaming hot cups onto the balcony and sat.

"So what are you making for supper?" Ed asked.

"The main course is a surprise, but for dessert I will be baking a special treat—my mother's apple pie."

"Terrific. Which reminds me, I've been meaning to ask you what your parents do, if you don't mind my asking?"

She shook her head, smiling. "Getting kind of personal aren't we?"

"Hey, if you don't want to . . ." but he was cut off short.

"No, that's fine. I actually appreciate your asking. My mother is, and always has been, a homemaker. And I've got to tell you, as much as I am a feminist and all that, it sure was nice to get home from school to have her there. So we are very close, and always have been."

"Good for your mum," he added.

"Well part of the reason she could stay home is that my father has always had a good job. They're not rich, but they've never wanted. In Canada, a ring on your pinkie usually results in a good job, especially in metallurgy."

Ed gave her a funny look. "Ring on pinkie? I thought that implied something else."

Pat thought about what he meant and burst out laughing. "You're thinking my dad is gay. That is funny. I'll be sure to tell him you said so,"

Ed laughed. "No don't do that. If I ever meet him, I don't want him thinking I'm ignorant. Although," he continued, "in this case I am."

She pulled her head back. "Why are you planning on meeting him?" she asked incredulously. Quickly she raised her hand. "No don't answer that. Let's stay away from that. What I meant is that he is an engineer. As a rule, engineers wear a thin ring on their small finger. Tradition I suppose. You're English; you should fully understand tradition—pip,

pip, and all that!" She added a fake English accent to get her point across.

He grinned, giving her the point. "Okay, you're right. Good day eh?"

She walked over to him, put a hand on either side of his head, leaned down, and kissed his forehead. "You're an okay guy, Ed. Maybe one day you will meet my parents. For now, I'm going to start working on that apple pie. Why don't you put some music on?"

He didn't need to ask what she wanted to hear. He found a Gordon Lightfoot tape and put it on. She thanked him with a wink as the first song started. He sat back in the chair listened to the words of the songs and watched Pat cook. She quietly hummed or sang with the songs. He closed his eyes and fell asleep.

He woke to the smell of apple pie, Pat standing in front of him in a different dress, and Gordon Lightfoot singing 'The First Time Ever I Saw Your Face'.

"Sorry, I nodded off," Ed said, sitting up and rubbing his eyes.

"By the way," Pat said, "you owe me a promise—or two."

Ed thought for a second. "Ah yes, as in . . . a promise made is a debt unpaid."

Pat motioned him to the balcony. She took a seat, and had him stand with his back to the view of Ottawa. It was getting dark and a chill was coming on. "Recite away," she said.

He bowed to his audience, coughed professionally, and began reciting 'The Shooting of Dan McGrew'.

She watched and listened to his inflections and interpretation of the poem. Not bad for a limey, she thought.

He finished the poem:

> 'The woman that kissed him and—pinched his poke—
> was the lady that's know as Lou.'

"Very good, Ed, very good," Pat said applauding. "You make a fine Canadian."

He bowed, acknowledging her applause.

"So the message," she said, "is—men are dumb; women are clever."

"I doubt that was Mr. Service's message," Ed laughed. "But it's difficult to argue against that point of view given the end result."

"Next," she said.

He took a deep breath, and began, *"There are strange things done in the midnight sun . . ."*

Pat watched and listened again, happy to have him recite the poem with such enthusiasm. He finished, pointing to the sky:

> *'The Northern Lights have seen queer sights, but the queerest they ever did see*
> *Was that night on the marge of Lake Labarge, I cremated Sam McGee.*

"Wonderful. That was so good."

They went inside. Pat made a quick decision, hoping it would work out to her advantage. She had to set the picture straight!

"C'mon join me at the table," Pat said. "There's a fresh cup of tea and I want to show you something."

Ed joined her at the table as she poured the tea. "You look very lovely in that dress, Pat."

"Thanks. It's one of my favorites."

"Is that what you wanted to show me?" Ed asked. "If it was, it was well worth it."

She shook her head, walked back to the kitchen area returning with the cooked apple pie and a pair of scissors. She removed a narrow strip of aluminum film from around the edge of the pie.

"Stops it from burning," she explained.

"Looks and smells great," Ed said.

Without speaking, she cut up a thin strip of the aluminum film rolled it, and then she twisted it into a ring. She took his left hand and put the ring on his little finger.

"There," she said, "now you're an engineer."

"Thank you. If only it were that easy." He held his hand out in front of him admiring his new ring.

"'If only' is right," she agreed. "Look, Ed, I have a question to ask you."

He lowered his hand. He could tell she was feeling awkward about herself. He nodded.

"Do you recall," she started, "when I was driving you back to Oakville the second time you came to Canada?"

"Oh yes, I recall. You were pretty put off. Ruining your long weekend, and you made that clear." He paused. "Am I . . ?"

"No, no. Hear me out. Do you remember asking me a question as we were driving?"

He remembered immediately. "Of course I do, I asked you to marry me." He was tempted to expand, but decided not to.

"Right," she smiled. "And I said something like 'not a bloody chance' or something like that."

He nodded. "Something close to that, yes."

She closed here eyes briefly, took a deep breath, and looked up at him. "Well I've changed my mind. I accept your offer of marriage." She tried to smile, but gulped to hold back a tear.

He took her hands in his. "Pat, you don't have to do this. I, we . . ."

She tried to take her hands away, but he held them firm. "Are you saying no, Ed?"

"No Pat, I'm not saying no." He took the ring from his little finger and placed it on her left hand. Then he lifted her hand and kissed the ring.

She coughed to clear her throat. "Thank you, Ed. Now I've been thinking . . ."

"Obviously."

She ignored the comment. "I've been thinking that since we're officially engaged, I'm not sure the department rules apply."

He nodded thoughtfully. "So perhaps it's okay if I kiss your forehead?"

"Probably."

"Maybe even kiss your neck? Kiss your lips even?"

She shrugged. "You'd think so, wouldn't you?"

"Hmm," he thought. "What about slowly unzipping your dress and massaging your lovely soft skin?"

She gulped. "Makes sense to me."

"Then it would only make sense that I, slowly mind you, remove your dress and have you standing in just your underwear?"

"My new sexy underwear, yes." She spoke quickly.

Now Ed gulped. "And it would follow Pat, that I remove you bra and kiss and lick your breasts. Would that make sense?"

"Oh Ed! All the sense in the world."

He leaned forward and kissed her forehead. She closed her eyes, imagining the rest. She took his hand and led him into her bedroom. She pulled the door partially closed and drew the curtains. She started by taking off his shirt. She grimaced at the bandages covering the entrance and exit holes of the bullet.

"They don't hurt any more," he said, looking down.

She was careful not to touch them and moved up, kissing his nipples. She looked up at him smiling as she gently bit his nipple. "That's a hint," she said.

"I'm changing the order," he said, asking her to turn around, which she did. He slowly lowered the zipper on her dress. He kissed her neck as he unclipped the top of her dress. "I'm going to make you come beautifully, Pat. Just do as I say."

She nodded, reaching back to feel him through his pants. He took off her dress, had her step out of it, and tossed it to one side. He had her bend over with her hands on the bed. Sliding his hand across her panties and between her legs he gently massaged her now moist area.

"That's lovely," she murmured, "so lovely."

Standing her up and turning her, he sat on the bed. He reached behind her and undid her bra. She wanted him to remove it quickly, but he slowly slid it off, exposing one breast at a time. Her nipples were firm and felt wonderful in his hands. Smiling up to her, he gently bit her right nipple and then her left. She felt wonderful, holding his head to her breasts.

Having him stand, she undid his belt and removed his pants. His swollen cock bulged through his shorts. Slipping to her knees, she carefully removed his shorts and held him with both hands. She kissed and licked the head of his cock, feeling his excitement as she did. After looking up at him and smiling, she put her mouth over his cock and in took as much as she could. She removed it from her mouth, licked it again, and stood up. "More of that later," she whispered.

He smiled. "That was wonderful. You almost made me come."

"I want you to come in me later, Ed. I want to feel you come in me. No condom, just you."

"That will be my pleasure. Let's get on the bed, Pat," he said, reaching under her panties and squeezing her cheeks. "I want to tease you a bit, and then I want desperately to fuck you."

"Yes sir," she grinned, "just show me what to do."

An hour later they were in the kitchen sipping on red wine. Pat was working on supper—Tandoori chicken—one of her favorites, and Ed was helping out by keeping the wine flowing. He watched her carefully, knowing that he needed to expand his culinary skills.

"You're beautiful naked, Pat, but that dress is very lovely."

"Thanks. It doesn't crease too easily when it's thrown across the room either."

"And you underwear is very sexy, by the way." He toasted her with his wine.

She put the chicken she was holding down. "Listen, you keep talking like that and I'll drag you back into the bedroom to you-know-what again."

He leaned over and whispered in her ear.

"Yes that," she confirmed.

After eating, they took their glasses of wine onto the balcony and enjoyed the view of Ottawa by night. Pat pointed out more historical buildings, and Ed learned more about his new country.

"Can I sleep with you tonight, Pat?" Ed asked as they walked into the apartment.

"No," she said with a twinkle in her eyes.

"Oh," was all he could muster.

"Look I don't want you to think I'm weird or anything, and it's awkward asking you this . . ."

"Ask away."

She grimaced. "I'd like you to enter my bedroom in the morning, and . . . and, well you know."

Ed nodded. "You want me to ravage your body? Gently like?" It wasn't a question, more of a statement. He smiled as he asked.

"Yeah, I guess so. I don't want you to hurt me or anything, it's just that . . ."

He put a finger to her lips. "You just get a good night's sleep. A good innocent night's sleep that is."

"Thanks," she said quickly and went into her bedroom.

CHAPTER FIFTEEN

SUNDAY, OCTOBER 14TH

• • ● ● ● ● •

"Whew, that was wicked," Pat said, turning onto her back in her bed to face him. "I'm glad I had the courage to ask for that."

Ed had entered her bedroom thirty minutes earlier and had gently ravaged her body. He had only spoken once, 'ordering' her to "Turn over." She was uncertain at the time that she wanted to do so; aware of what he was going to do. He had raised her up and massaged her until she was moist and ready for him. He then entered her from behind and pumped into her until she groaned in pleasure and pulled away from him. Now she knew she would do it again, if the occasion arose. She smiled at the thought.

He took a deep breath. "Of course 'gentle ravage' is a bit of an oxymoron isn't it?"

"It may well be," she said, kissing his chin, "but it sure felt good to me."

She pulled the top sheet over them, and moved closer to him. "Hold me close, Ed." He pulled her into his body, spreading his hands across her back. They didn't move or speak of a couple of minutes.

"I want to remember us like this." She whispered, more than spoke.

"So do I," Ed agreed.

She pushed herself and sat halfway up. She slowly took off the ring, and turned to him.

"I have to cancel our engagement, Ed," she smiled. "I'm returning your ring."

He sat up and took the ring. "You can keep it if you like."

"No, I'd get sad every time I looked at it. You keep it. Or throw it away if you like."

He frowned at the thought. "No, Pat, I'm going to keep it. In fact I'm going to keep it in my wallet. When I look at it, I will always think of us as we are now."

"Naked and happy," she laughed.

"Naked, happy, and very good friends."

"Even better," she agreed. "Now go back to your bedroom. I'm first in the shower."

Leaning over, he kissed her forehead and then left her room.

Ed's bag was by the door to the hallway. He had packed, appreciative of a week's clean underwear. The ring was safely in his wallet. Pat had cooked a large breakfast, leaving plenty of time to get him to the train station.

"You have to travel by train to be a true Canadian," Pat had said, giving him his ticket. "It goes directly to Oakville. You don't have to change at Toronto."

"What do I owe you?" Ed asked.

"Nothing. It's complimentary of the Canadian taxpayer. Enjoy some of your taxes."

She ushered him to the chesterfield. She sat next to him, holding his hands in hers. "Now I have two questions for you Ed."

"Okay, I'm all ears."

"First question. Would you be interested in our renting a boat and cruising in it from Ottawa to Oakville and back via the Rideau Canal? Sometime in the summer, June maybe?"

"Absolutely and completely," he said, excitedly. "My only question is who'd be the captain?"

"We'd arm wrestle for it!" She was thrilled at his response.

"Let's make it fair, we'll flip for it just before we cast off."

"Okay, I'll look up some rental places in the next few weeks. Pencil it in for first week of June."

"Done," he said, touching his head with a finger, and then retuning his hand to hers.

"Second question. Can you dance?'

He looked at her questioningly. She nodded her head to confirm the question.

"Yes, I've actually taken ballroom dancing lessons. I'm not very good, but I won't step on your toes you either."

"Good," she said, walking to the tape deck. She pressed the button. "Please dance with me, Ed."

He took her in his arms and they danced slowly to Gordon Lightfoot's *Looking at the Rain*.

"Listen to the words, Ed."

He did, and looking down at her he smiled. "I get the point, Pat."

"Good. He's better at expressing himself than I am." She hugged into him, and then looked up. "I want to say something, Ed, and I don't want you to respond. Please don't say a word." He agreed by nodding.

She spoke quietly but quickly. "I love you, Ed. I need you to know that. I've never said that to a man before, and I am so happy that I can say it for the first time to my first real lover." She looked down and pressed her face to his body. "Now just dance, okay?"

The song ended, she broke away from him and turned off the music.

"So," she asked nervously, "do you want to cancel the cruise?"

He shook his head. "No, I think we should book it this week!"

She closed her eyes briefly, happy that she had taken the risk. "You know for a shoot-now-and-ask-questions-later kind of guy, you're not too bad."

"Hey, that's a bit unfair," he laughed.

"Two men in two weeks. Seems like a fair statement to me! Beside, who says life is fair?"

"Not your father as I recall."

"Exactly. Now let's get out of here and get you to your train."

He picked up his bag, and they left the apartment arm in arm.

Pat couldn't help but smile as she drove back to her apartment after dropping Ed off at the train station. She was aware that soon, very soon perhaps, her mother would, once more, start dropping subtle hints about Pat's lack of male friends; not liking the term 'boy friends'. Pat could now state categorically and truthfully that she had met a man she loved; that they will be going on vacation together, but the chances of them becoming serious was slim. It was accurate and she allowed herself to take great pleasure in it. She smiled all the way home.

Ed enjoyed the train ride back to Oakville, spending most of the time wondering what had occurred that resulted in such a change in Pat. He knew he liked her, liked her a great deal. He had to ensure that he was in no way responsible for hurting Pat's feelings. He had to think the entire matter through. He had plenty of time to sort it out—June was a very long way off.

CHAPTER SIXTEEN

WEDNESDAY, OCTOBER 24ᵀᴴ

• • • • • • •

Diane, the owner of the travel agency, and Ed's boss, closed the meeting by reminding everyone that Christmas travel season would soon be moving into full gear. Ed walked back to his office, coffee cup in hand, wanting to learn more about where the popular tourist spots for Canadians at Christmas were. He didn't have to be told that it was none of Turkey, Libya, or Bulgaria. After topping up his cup, he sat at his desk and starting flipping through the flyers, magazines, and ads for the Christmas travel season.

Diane entered his office, closed the door partly behind her, and gave a puzzled look.

"There's a lady in the front that insists on seeing you, Ed. Could it be you mother, she's very English?"

"Not a chance," Ed laughed. "I'll clean up my desk. Why don't you bring her . . . ?"

The door being pushed open interrupted him, and Diane stepped aside.

"No need to clean up your desk, Mr. Crowe. I haven't the time for formalities." Lady Stonebridge made her entrance undeniably memorable.

Ed motioned that everything was okay to Diane, and addressed his guest with utmost charm.

"Lady Stonebridge, what an unexpected and pleasant surprise," he smiled. "Please sit down."

She sat, first ensuring that the door was closed. She wore a fashionable winter coat and winter boots that were too early for the temperature.

She looked around the office, almost disapprovingly. "This is a rather small office, Mr. Crowe. Are rent prices so high in Toronto?" She pronounced it 'Tor-on-toe'.

"Higher than you might think, Lady Stonebridge. It's not London or New York, but like any big city . . ." He didn't finish the sentence.

"And I suppose you have to heat it during your terrible winters?"

"I suppose so. I have yet to experience one."

"Yes, well I do hope it goes well." She put her hands on her lap. "But of course, Mr. Crowe, I have not come to talk to you about the weather, have I?"

"I assume not."

"My husband is in Washington talking about whatever people in his business talk about, and I took the opportunity to fly up to Toronto to meet with you. I realize I should have phoned first, but didn't."

Ed shrugged, accepting the facts for what they were. "How may I help you, Lady Stonebridge?"

She looked around the room, obviously not feeling comfortable.

"My plan was not to disturb you at work, Mr. Crowe. I would like to meet with you more privately. May I buy you dinner to-night, or perhaps you have some kind of date?"

"Just a bit o' bubble and squeak and watching Corrie Street on the ol' telly." He smiled. "I'd be pleased to join you for dinner Lady Stonebridge."

She returned the smile. "Point taken, Mr. Crowe. Where would you like to go? I'm being driven by two friends of yours, Sergeants Tyson and McDowell. Location is not a problem."

"Then I'd suggest The Queen's Head; say six-thirty?"

"I take it that is a pub?"

"And a very fine one at that," he answered.

"I am impressed. Do they serve Guinness?"

"For those that have acquired the taste, they most certainly do."

"Then I shall see you at six-thirty." Lady Stonebridge stood, tipped her head, and left.

Diane popped her head in. "Who the hell is that? I thought I'd recognize the Queen of England when I saw her."

"She's the mother of a friend. Not quite royalty, but getting up there."

Diane leaned forward and whispered. "I don't know where you go on these trips of yours, but I'm more impressed by the minute."

She left Ed's office, closing the door reverently behind her.

Ed had just ordered his Double Diamond when Lady Stonebridge entered the pub. She saw him at the bar and joined him,

"First things first, Mr. Crowe, may I call you Edwin? It is your name I believe."

"I'd prefer Ed, but . . ."

"What does your mother call you?"

"Edwin."

"Then I'm sure she had a reason to do so. I shall call you Edwin."

He nodded. No sense arguing.

"And what do your friends call your mother?"

"Usually Mrs. 'C'."

"Then please refer to me as Mrs. 'S'."

Ed smiled. "Perhaps I should call you Mrs. 'C'?" He nodded knowingly.

"Let's keep my husband's business out of this shall we?"

"Yes, of course Mrs. 'S', very wise." It had struck him that with Lord Stonebridge being the head of MI6, and that role normally referred to as 'C', that his idea was a clever one. Obviously she did not agree.

Karen put Ed's pint on the bar, and turned to Lady Stonebridge. "Madam?"

"I'll have a half pint of Guinness please," she said, "and if Edwin's beer is not paid for yet, please add it to my bill."

Karen gave Ed a quick look. "Add Edwin's to your bill; no problem madam."

Karen slowly pulled the Guinness.

"Do you know what they sometimes call Guinness?" Lady Stonebridge asked.

Neither Ed nor Karen knew.

"Irish oil," Lady Stonebridge answered.

"Because of the taste?" Ed asked.

He got a dirty look from Lady Stonebridge as she took the drink from Karen. "Were you born in England?" she asked Karen.

Karen shook her head. "No, but my parents were born in Luton."

"Ah, yes I know it well. I was born and raised in Neasden."

Karen shook her head. "Don't know it I'm afraid."

"It's just south of St. Albans," Lady Stonebridge said.

"And just north of Kilburn," Ed added.

"Oh, I've been to St. Albans," Karen said, smiling. "It's a lovely town to visit. But I've never heard of Kilburn."

"No reason you would have," Lady Stonebridge said, giving Ed a cold look. "Not exactly a tourist haven is Kilburn."

Ed looked at Karen. "Mrs. 'S' is in from England. She's the mother of a lady friend of mine."

Karen nodded. "Yes, I thought I could see the similarity. Dry red wine, right?"

"That's the lady," Ed agreed, happy she hadn't said 'Bloody Caesar'—Pat's regular drink.

"Shall we take a seat?" Ed asked, picking up both drinks. He gave Karen an approving nod and followed Lady Stonebridge to a table in the corner, well away from the bar.

After reviewing the menu, they ordered. Ed recommended the fish special, Scottish Haddock and chips.

"I am complimented that the lady at the bar saw some Carolyn in me," Lady Stonebridge said proudly. "While as her mother I may perhaps be jaded, I do believe she is quite pretty."

"She most certainly is," Ed agreed.

"One of the reasons I flew to Toronto today," Lady Stonebridge continued, "is to thank you personally for your most courageous role in helping in the return of Carolyn to my husband and myself. It is difficult to explain how terrible we felt as parents, having no control over the events that took place. As independent and as self-assured as she is, to us she is still our baby daughter. Please accept my sincere thanks, Edwin. It's not often that words fail me, but today . . ."

Ed waited for Lady Stonebridge to collect herself before he replied. "I'm a little at a loss for words my self actually. I want to say it was my pleasure, but that trivializes both the risk Carolyn was in, and the risk I took in my actions. Let us just be happy that things worked out as well as they did. I do appreciate your taking the time to drop by personally. Are you staying long?" He wanted to change the discussion.

"And since we are discussing Carolyn, may I ask when you last spoke to her?"

"That would be just before I was arrested, in Sofia."

"Not since? I am surprised."

"Not since, no."

Lady Stonebridge thought for a moment. "Are you going to make my asking these questions more difficult for me than it already is, Edwin?"

Ed shook his head. "No, Lady Stonebridge, that is not my goal at all. I might, perhaps, be endeavoring to make answering your questions easier for me, and that is an entirely different scenario."

"I can understand that perspective, Edwin. Perhaps if you would be good enough to consider my being here as the scenario of Carolyn being my daughter instead of my being her mother, it might shed some light on the matter."

Ed nodded. "Of course, please proceed. I apologize for thinking more of myself than Carolyn. How can I help you Lady . . ."

"Mrs. 'S'," she interrupted.

"How can I help you Mrs. 'S'?"

"Thank you, Edwin. Could I ask why you have not contacted her? You know she is in Paris at the Embassy. Not a difficult telephone number to find, I am sure."

Ed swallowed, and took a deep breath. "Mrs. 'S', you gave me a letter from Carolyn. Without going into the details, let me say that the letter made it clear that she did not want me to keep in contact with her. You are aware that I love Carolyn, I've told you so myself. Surely it is not unusual to not only love someone, but also respect her desire? I can accept what she wrote with great sadness. I cannot, in fact will not, phone her—just to have her hang-up on me or offer words to that effect. That would truly break my heart." He paused and swallowed again. "With great respect Mrs. 'S', you are making this very awkward."

"Yes, the letter," she said sadly. "Did you read the letter, Edwin?"

"Of course I did, as best I could anyway."

She shrugged her confusion.

"I had only the time to skim the letter, and then your husband, Lord Stonebridge, whatever . . ."

"Whomever," she corrected him.

He rubbed his chin to slow down. "Then 'whomever' let me know that Carolyn had been kidnapped. You know the rest from there."

"And you read the letter in full at a later date then?"

He squirmed slightly in the chair. "Actually, no. I'm afraid in all the confusion I lost the letter."

"I see," she said. "Most unfortunate."

"I prefer to think of the contents of the letter as most unfortunate, not the fact that I lost it."

"Oh, you did not lose the letter, Edwin, I have it right here in my handbag."

Ed rolled his eyes and raised his hands in utter confusion. "What am I to say?" he mumbled. "You could have simply mailed it to me, and I could read it and weep. A fine ending to a short friendship I am sure."

"I could have done so, if that was my only goal. What I would much prefer, is that you read it here . . . and now."

Ed couldn't think of what to say or do. He simply stared at her with a blank look on his face.

"What are you thinking, Edwin?"

"I suspect the word is 'wicked'," he replied, trying not to sound overly rude.

The waitress brought their food. "Another drink?' she asked them.

"Oh yes please," Ed said, finishing his beer in a gulp. Lady Stonebridge passed.

They ate their meals in silence. Ed took his time, forcing himself to calm his manner. The waitress delivered his beer. He intentionally did not drink any of it, he wanted to remain calm.

Not until all of the plates had been taken away and the table was empty, except for their drinks, did the conversation continue.

"Would you prefer that I read it out loud?" Ed asked politely.

She smiled. "Actually I would prefer that, but I think it will be easier for you to read it to yourself. I will order myself a glass of wine. Dry red, I believe?" She gave him the envelope, as she raised her hand to catch the waitress's attention.

Ed took out the letter and read it slowly—to himself.

> *Dear Ed*
>
> *I have been thinking about our relationship, and how we might proceed in view of our significantly different lifestyles and backgrounds. Please excuse my typing this letter. I find it easier to document matters for clarity sake. Perhaps my civil service training?*
>
> *I have subsequently had time to reflect on our discussions, and in particular the point you raised in regard to my attending Royal Ascot and how distant a world that*

is, as you so correctly pointed out, from that of yours and your mother's. (A wonderful person let me add.) While I might be inclined to take no note of these sort of matters, it strikes me that you would find doing so more complicated than I. I recall we agreed on the premise that we will—and please excuse the words—not grow old together. I am most reluctant to continue expecting your love and kindness, and in doing so deny it to another. Love such as yours cannot be shared. It must grow and bloom, and indeed must multiply. I readily leave the continuation of our friendship in your safe and reliable hands.

I hope you have a wonderful life should we not cross paths again.

Ed folded the letter, replaced it in the envelope, and offered it back to Lady Stonebridge.

She shook her head. "The letter is yours, not mine."

"I assume you have read it?"

"More than that, I typed it."

Ed looked at her, and chuckled. "Really?"

"I typed it, Edwin, I didn't dictate it. Carolyn did. Typing is not a skill one is taught in school any more," she smiled. "And besides, Carolyn did ask for my help in drafting the letter. A great compliment to me I can assure you, given our sometimes awkward relationship."

Ed rubbed his forehead, trying to understand the implications of what was happening. He thought for a while. Lady Stonebridge sipped on her wine.

He turned to Lady Stonebridge, not sure how to address his question. "There's something in the letter that I don't quite understand."

"Can you be more specific?"

"I'm trying to be anything but specific. In fact in today's parlance I would say I'm trying to cover my ass!"

"Ah the reference to Pat?"

Ed sat back, amazed. "There is no reference to Pat for crying out loud!"

"But of course there is, Edwin. It's just that her name is not mentioned."

He bit his lip, now lost to the process. He felt cornered, yet comfortably cornered. "You're too wily for me Mrs. 'S'. You know more than I know you know, and I don't know how much more you know."

"What I know doesn't matter. You've read the letter. You better understand its intent. My job here is done."

"May I ask a couple of questions then?"

"Of course."

"Does Carolyn know you are here?"

"Certainly not. If she were to find out she would not speak to me again. Nor to you I might wonder."

"I know Pat and Carolyn chatted . . ."

She shook her head. "I cannot speak to that. Just let it be understood that women are, by their very nature, more honest amongst themselves than are men."

"Thus ends the conversation?" Ed mused.

"On that point, yes."

"One final question Mrs. 'S'. Why or how did the letter get back to you?"

"Ah yes, an important question. The simple answer is that Carolyn changed her mind. She did not want you to see the letter and have you make the decision not to see her further. So I had Mr. Williams from the Embassy retrieve it for me: all very unofficial of course. When you did not contact her, she naturally assumed you had read the letter and made your decision."

"Of course, and now she's mad at me."

"She is mad at herself, Edwin. She is not herself at all. With the kidnapping, and now this . . . ." She didn't finish the sentence.

"So where do we go from here?" Ed asked.

"Well I will pay the bill, have those two nice men drive me to the airport and be back in Washington before my husband misses me. Where you go from here, is of course your own choice. Today I wanted to thank you and make sure you had in fact read the letter. My job, as it were, is done." She called for the bill.

After paying the bill, leaving a generous tip in the process, she shook Ed's hand, and left.

Ed carried his still half full beer to the bar. After Karen had finished serving other customers, she leaned over to Ed.

"Quite a lady?" she said, wiping the bar.

"In more ways than one." He leaned forward. "Thanks, by the way, for getting the drink right."

"Could hardly miss her accent, could I?" She smiled. "Although I was tempted . . ."

He rolled his eyes. "Lead us not into temptation . . ."

He was tempted to have a third beer, but took his own advice and went home.

He was sitting thinking about what had happened when the phone rang. He recognized Pat's voice immediately.

"Hey, how's it going?" Her voice was bubbly.

"Hey yourself, Pat. Fine and yourself?"

"Never better. Listen, it took me a while but I finally got the information on renting a boat in June. Still interested?"

"Sure, fine idea."

She paused before she replied. "That sounds like a total lack of enthusiasm. Have I got you on a bad day?"

"Sorry, Pat. I've just got a few things on my mind."

Her enthusiasm had disappeared. She spoke slowly. "Look, Ed, if it's what I said the other week?"

He felt like kicking himself. "No, honest. It's just . . ."

"Hang on here, let me speak." She interrupted and her voice was now cold. "What I said I meant. But I don't want you thinking that I'm trying to force you or embarrass you into anything that you don't want to do. Shit, Ed, that hurts!"

"No Pat, listen. Don't hang up. There's some family stuff going on in England," he lied. "I do want us to rent the boat. Forgive me, please?" No response. "Pretty please?"

"Don't bull-shit me here, Ed."

"I wouldn't dream of bull-shitting you, Pat. What's the deal? Dates, price, etc."

She was excited again. "Okay, here's the scoop . . ."

She outlined the information she had gathered, and they agreed on dates, the type of boat, and the many details involved. She agreed to work on the details and get back to him the following week.

He made a note on his calendar for the next day: 'Send Pat flowers!'

CHAPTER SEVENTEEN

THURSDAY, OCTOBER 25ᵀᴴ

• • • ● ● ● • •

Diane wasn't sure whether to be surprised or not. "So this fancy lady takes you out for supper and now you have to fly off to Paris! That's pretty interesting."

"I'll be back by Tuesday. I'm sure it won't take any longer," Ed said, not wanting to push his special status too far.

"Hey ya gotta go, ya gotta go, right?"

"Great. Can I bring you anything back from Paris?"

Diane thought for a second. "A nice, rich Frenchman would be nice."

Ed looked at her, pulling a face.

"Yeah, you're right," she said. "That's a contradiction in terms!"

Ed returned to his office, made some changes to his calendar and left for Toronto International airport.

CHAPTER EIGHTEEN

FRIDAY, OCTOBER 26TH

• • • • • • •

The Air Canada flight arrived on time at Charles de Gaulle International Airport. It was seven-thirty a.m. local time. Ed had tried unsuccessfully to sleep. His nerves were too on edge for relaxation. The passport process was quick and friendly. Perhaps the French are not as pompous as their reputation, he thought. He carried only a small bag, with enough clothes to see him for a couple of days. He converted cash into French Francs, and was on his way.

The Taxi was small compared to most cities he had visited, and he had never seen a dog accompanying a driver before. The dog sat in the front passenger seat. It was small and quiet. Not built for protection, Ed was sure of that.

"Oui?" the driver asked.

"Hotel Moderne, place de Republic," Ed explained, trying to pronounce it in French.

The look on the driver's face told him he had not done well.

The registration into the hotel appeared to drag him back to the past. There did not seem to be any form of computerization, and if there was any, it was well hidden. On the other hand, the room was huge with fifteen-foot ceilings and a bed that could hold four people. That made him wonder, but he put it out of his mind. He unpacked what little he had. His clothes didn't even fill the smallest of the drawer in the massive chest-of-drawers. To make himself feel better he separated his socks from his underwear and used two drawers. He sensed he would get his money's worth now!

The drive to the British Embassy took them through the heart of Paris, and try as he might the driver did not hit another vehicle. Throughout the fist waving and shouts through the window, both the dog and Ed tried to relax. It worked for the dog. He paid the driver, tipping him enough so as to not be the recipient of any verbal abuse. It evidently worked. The driver thanked him and tipped his beret with a not too often seen smile.

Ed got out of the taxi and looked around. The Embassy was in a beautiful area of Paris. The avenue it was on was wide with many large trees to soften the tall and elegant buildings. The embassy was itself a massive building, probably twice the size of the embassy in Ankara. He was tempted to look around, but he knew he was simply putting off the inevitable. He looked at his watch. It was just gone ten a.m., as good a time as any. He entered the embassy; head up and shoulders back.

If the size of the reception area was intended to display wealth and history, it worked well. The ceiling, high above, was painstakingly ornate and regal. He looked up endeavoring to determine the message in the paintings.

"You'll get a sore neck," a female voice said.

He looked down and across the massive room. Some fifty feet away sat a young lady at an appropriately sized desk. He walked over, smiling as he did.

"Lovely place," he said. "Must set you back a bit!"

She smiled. "It's just taxpayers' money. Not real money."

He reached the desk, still admiring the surroundings.

"How can I help you, sir?" the receptionist asked.

"I would like to see Miss Andrews please." He spoke casually, but felt nervous.

"Yes, sir. Do you have an appointment?"

He smiled. "Not really."

"Not really, sir?"

"Perhaps the answer is 'no' then."

"Yes, sir. Who can I say wants to see her?"

He took a breath. "Pigeon."

"Yes, sir. Pigeon as in bird sir?"

"As in sitting duck, yes."

She looked somewhat confused, but picked up the phone and dialed.

"Miss Andrews, there's a gentleman to see you. A Mr. Pigeon." She paused. "Yes, Miss, as in bird." She looked at Ed smiling as she listened. She nodded and turned to Ed. "Miss Andrews would like to know if the Pigeon is related to the crow."

"Is that crow or Crowe?"

The receptionist shook her head and went back to the phone. "Mr. Pigeon would like to know if you mean crow or crow?" She listened, shrugged her shoulders, and turned back to Ed. "She means the one with an 'e' at the end."

"Alas, yes."

"Alas, yes, Miss."

Ed bit his bottom lip, watching for the eyes of the receptionist who nodded into the phone and put the phone gently on its cradle.

"Miss Andrews says she is too busy to see you now, Mr. Pigeon, and can you come back Monday please."

"She didn't?"

"She did."

"Monday. That's three days from now."

She counted slowly on her fingers. "Yes, that's three days from now."

He turned and started walking very slowly to the front door. He hadn't anticipated this. Now what? He didn't have a plan B.

A phone rang behind him and the receptionist answered it.

"Oh, Mr. Pigeon," she called to him. "Miss Andrews has managed to make some changes and she'll be down in a couple of minutes."

He made a silent prayer and walked back toward the reception desk. He took a seat the receptionist offered and waited. And waited. He didn't look at his watch, but it had to be ten minutes and no Miss Andrews. He smiled at the receptionist, who smiled back.

"Big building," he commented.

"Fresh make-up," she responded.

Ed stood and faced the direction of the sound of steps. The sound made only by a lady's high heels. Carolyn turned from the hallway into the reception area, and waved at the receptionist. "Good morning again, Terri," she said. She turned to Ed. "Good morning, Mr. Crowe. How are you this morning?"

Terri's eyes were wide open, but she said nothing.

"Good morning, Miss Andrews. I appreciate your seeing me on short notice."

"That would be no-notice I believe."

"Correct," Ed agreed.

Carolyn looked at Terri. "Mr. Crowe and I have met before."

Terri rolled her eyes. "Really? I would have never guessed."

Carolyn continued. "Mr. Crowe is from Canada."

"Yes, I could tell by the accent," Terri said sarcastically.

"Sharp tongue has our Terri," Carolyn added.

"I was born in London," Ed said. "Moved to Canada this year."

"I have a sister in Vancouver," Terri said. "Am I supposed to ask you if you know her?"

"Only if you're Irish," Ed replied quickly.

"Touché, Mr. Crowe," Terri said, smiling.

Carolyn turned to Ed, maintaining her professional manner. "How may I help you?"

"I would like to register as a British citizen please."

"This is Paris, Mr. Crowe, not Ankara. I'd suspect the risks are considerably fewer here."

Ed thought quickly "I understood some of the local citizens still resent the fact that the English saved them from the Nazis. Would that not put me at risk?"

Terri offered help. "He's got you there, Miss Andrews. Heck he's both English and Canadian. That could be double jeopardy!" She grinned, and handed Carolyn a blank registration form.

"Over here then, Mr. Crowe," Carolyn said, pointing to a desk and chairs off to the side. They sat across from each other.

"Seems like I've been here before," Ed said, looking directly at Carolyn.

"What are you doing in Paris, Ed?"

"I've come to see you, Carolyn."

"Shouldn't you have phoned? I do have a life you know?"

"You may have said 'No'. I couldn't take the risk."

"This is awkward, Ed. You've put me on the spot, and now you have a member of my staff batting for you."

"She's very intelligent."

"She's single if you're interested," Carolyn said bluntly.

Ed leaned closer. "Carolyn, please. Don't say things like that."

She gently shook her head. "Go left outside the front door. Take the first left and walk to the Champs-Elysees. Turn right toward the Arc de Triomphe. Find a restaurant and I'll join you in an hour."

"What's the restaurant's name?"

"There are a hundred of them. Pick one on this side of the street and sit on the patio. Don't worry, I'll be there."

"Terrific, I'll see you there." He got up to leave.

"And, Ed," she called after him, "drink the coffee slowly. This isn't Ankara."

He waved to Terri and left.

He aimlessly took Carolyn's directions, deep in thought as he strolled through the City of Lights. He hadn't expected her to jump in his arms, but neither had he expected so business-like a response. His mind cleared somewhat as he reached the Champs-Elysees. It was wider than any street in London, except perhaps for The Mall that leads to Buckingham Palace. But parks on either side did not protect this walkway. It was filled with shops, shoppers, and many restaurants. He took a table for two on the patio of a restaurant that offered a view of the Arc de Triomphe. He ordered a cup of coffee and now understood what Carolyn meant. The price was eight francs, or two dollars for cup of coffee. He drank it slowly.

He was still sipping on his first coffee when Carolyn joined him. She sat and ordered a coffee, in French.

"Bon jour," he tried in French.

"Bon jour yourself," she answered.

"Look maybe I've made a bit of a mess of this, Carolyn, and for that I do apologize." He had leaned closer to speak.

"I don't like being taken for granted," she replied, thanking the waiter as she spoke.

"Point taken. But can I see you tonight? I do need to talk to you."

"I have plans for tonight, Ed." She sipped her coffee. "Good coffee."

"What about tomorrow . . ."

She interrupted. "I have plans for the entire weekend, Ed."

"Oh," he mumbled. "I really blew this one didn't I?"

"Would you like to know who I'm seeing this weekend?" She kept her eyes fixed to his.

"I presume it's a guy. Have you known him long?"

"Not really, but we're quite close."

Ed swallowed and chewed on his lip. "Okay, I get the message. Look I'm sorry."

"He's from London," Carolyn continued, keeping her tone cool.

"Hey, I can take a hint, Carolyn. Let me pay for the coffee, and we'll call it even okay?" He stood.

"And," she said; now speaking louder, "he doesn't respond to personal letters written to him from his friend. What kind of a person is that, Ed?" People turned to look.

Ed sat back down. "Only a complete and absolute arsehole," he said, now grinning. "A total arsehole for sure."

She now spoke quietly. "Obviously you know of him?"

"Just a guy in my past," he said. "Hope to never see him again."

"Well we agree on that point." She picked up her coffee and smiled. "It's nice to see you, Ed. What does bring you to Paris?"

"I came to tell you I love you."

"Okay, now what?"

He reached over and took her hand. "You're not going to make this easy are you?"

"Should I?" She withdrew her hand and picked up her coffee.

"It's not like you think, Carolyn. Let me buy you dinner tonight. I would like to be the arsehole that shares the weekend with you."

"I think it's fair to say, Edwin Crowe, that you are the only a-hole I know in Paris."

"That's good then is it?"

She finished her coffee, took money from her purse and left it on the table. "My treat." She stood, snapping her handbag closed. "I have to get back to work."

Ed followed her out. "Can I walk with you to the embassy?"

"It's a public street."

He walked beside her, dodging the teeming shoppers and tourists.

"Can I hold your hand, Carolyn?" he asked, making way for a very well dressed lady who was carrying her dog.

"Certainly not."

They turned left onto a less busy street.

"May I ask why not?"

"You may." She continued walking.

"Okay, I give up. Why not?"

She stopped and turned to him. "Because Senior Intelligence Officers of The Foreign Office do not walk down the street holding hands."

He grinned. "Is that a promotion?"

"Does that surprise you?" She started walking again and he ran to keep up.

"Absolutely not. Congratulations. Can I buy you dinner as a celebratory treat?"

"Perhaps."

He leaned closer to her. "Do you know we're being followed?"

"Of course I know. They're ours."

"Protection for you?"

"Sort of. They're new at the job."

"Will they be watching when I kiss you goodnight after our date?"

They stopped at the door to the embassy. The two men kept walking and passed them.

"Who said anything about kissing?" Carolyn asked.

"I did," he smirked. "But I don't want them shooting me for a kiss!"

"Not everyone's as trigger-happy as you, Ed." She smiled nicely.

"Ouch, that hurt!" He put his hand to his heart.

"Which reminds me," she said, "I'd like to thank you for saving me in Sofia, and would ask you to join me at my apartment tomorrow night for a meal."

"I'd be delighted, Carolyn."

"Okay, I've got to go. Which hotel are you staying at?"

He told her.

"I'll be there at six. Be ready."

She put her hand out, which he shook.

"May I kiss you tonight?" he asked, not letting go of her hand.

"That, Mr. Crowe," she replied with a grin, "is for me to know, and for you to find out!"

She turned and entered the embassy.

He set the alarm for five, giving himself an hour to get ready for Carolyn. He was content and happy. He smiled as his head touched the pillow, and he was asleep in less than a minute.

The banging on the door woke him with a start. The clock showed four thirty-five. Jumping up, he ran to the bathroom, wrapped a towel around his waist, and walked to the door. He opened it carefully, ready to jump back if he needed to. He peeked through the gap.

"Are you going to let me in?" Carolyn asked.

He opened the door fully. She entered and looked around. "Nice room. Did you get the government rate?"

"It's not government business. I thought you were going to be here at six?"

"I left early. It'll help Terri's rumor mill about some good looking Canadian with a cockney accent and a funny name."

"I don't think Crowe's a funny name!"

"Then you tell Terri."

She sat on the bed, bouncing on it to check. "Let me see your scars please."

He walked over to her, holding onto the towel. He turned for her to see the two healed scars. She touched them gently. "Do they hurt?"

"Not now, no."

She moved his hand from the towel, unhooked it, and let it fall to the ground. He was beginning to get an erection. She looked up at him and then back to his erection. It was now firm and straight. She gently touched the head of his cock. She stood up.

"You can put that away," she smiled pointing to his erection.

"What?" Ed exclaimed. "Jesus, you're making it a rough day for me."

She shrugged her shoulders. "Tough all the way around, eh? Put some clothes on, and let's go."

He grabbed underwear and clothes and walked naked into the bathroom. "Where are we going," he asked through the door as he brushed his teeth.

"Somewhere expensive," she called back. "I'm going to make you pay for what you did to me."

He gargled and spat it out. "Okay with me. Nothing's cheap in Paris anyway." He walked back into the main room.

Carolyn was standing next to the bed, wearing only her bra and panties. Her business suit was hung neatly on the chair. Her arms were by her side.

"You look lovely," Ed said.

"Thank you," Carolyn replied. "You're over-dressed."

He waked over to her and stopping three feet away, took in her beautiful figure. "Your nipples are hard," he said smiling.

"They're cold."

"They must be very cold," he said, now taking her in his arms. "I'll warm them up with my tongue if you like?"

She clung onto him. "That would be very nice, Ed." She pushed him back slightly. "I want to undress you," she said, un-buttoning his shirt.

She slowly undressed him, folding his clothes neatly as she did. When he was down to just his shorts, she took his hand and led him onto the bed.

They caressed and kissed each other slowly and carefully. When they could bear it no longer, they removed each others remaining clothes. She gently took his cock in her mouth, licking it as she held him in. He moved down to her now moist spot kissing and licking her. When she pushed his head gently, he opened her and forced his tongue in her as deeply as he could. She groaned in delight, held him down and then pulled his head up to her breasts.

Reaching down she took his cock in her hand. "I want you in me; now."

He entered her wanting to move quickly but knowing how much she enjoyed the delay, he took his time moving in and out slowly. Opening her eyes and smiling she whispered, "Faster please, Ed." He moved faster and then faster until he knew he could delay no longer. He exploded in her, she came in delight, and the alarm clock went off.

She giggled with delight as he struggled to turn off the alarm clock. "Not quite saved by the bell," she said.

He rolled back to her and they held on to each other as if for the first time.

"Without sounding like a sixties song," Carolyn said, "have I told you lately that I love you?"

"Now that you mention it, no you haven't." He kissed her breast and then kissed her other breast. She stroked his head as he kissed her.

"I wanted us to make love before you tell me what happened," Carolyn said. "Just in case I don't believe you."

"You will," he said sitting up. "It's too impossible not to be true."

"Good. I'm looking forward to hearing the details. The reservation is for six-thirty."

"Before we go, can I ask a favor of you?"

She nodded.

"Can we spend the entire weekend together? I mean go to bed together, get up in the morning together, and spend the entire time together?"

"Like an old married couple?" she asked with a smile.

"Sort of, I suppose. Although I wouldn't use the word 'old' quite yet."

"Of course we can," she said leaning over to kiss him. "Maybe we could even shower together?"

"Yes, that would be perfect."

"How about right now?"

"No time like the present!" he agreed.

Carolyn conversed easily with the taxi driver in French. During the conversation she looked at Ed as she spoke.

"What are you saying about me?" Ed asked.

"He wants to know why you don't speak French," Carolyn replied.

"Does he speak English?"

"We're not in England are we?"

"Very clever," Ed said. "Ask him if it mattered that the soldiers from the Allied forces didn't speak French when they came to rescue France in 1944?"

"Don't take offense so easily. He's French. Even worse he's from Paris. He thinks he's special."

The driver was smiling into the rear view mirror.

"So ask him," Ed said, smiling back into the mirror.

Carolyn shrugged and spoke to the driver. The driver's face turned red and he let go a barrage of words directed at them along with a variety of hand gestures. Ed was worried he would lose control of the car.

"So what did he say?" Ed asked.

"Amongst other things, he made it clear that many French people died in the war, and many more suffered at the hands of the Nazis. He also had some suggestions for Mrs. Thatcher that I won't expand on."

"So perhaps we shouldn't mention the V-I-C-H-Y government to the driver then?" Ed asked, satisfied with the result so far.

"Perhaps not, eh!" Carolyn agreed.

There was a cold silence in the taxi until it arrived at the restaurant. Carolyn paid the driver to eliminate any further discussion.

The restaurant was small and cozy. Ed liked it right away.

"We're the only customers," he said, looking around.

"The French don't usually eat until eightish. But if it's okay with you, I'm hungry and I feel more secure with fewer people around."

"Fine by me. I'm famished."

They were seated away in a corner, as far as was possible away from the entrance and the doorway to the kitchen.

"We could make love here, and nobody would know," Ed said.

"I'd know."

"God, I hope so."

The waiter left the menus and Carolyn ordered a bottle of wine. They kept their conversation light until the wine was delivered and poured.

"To new friends," Ed offered.

"To special new friends," Carolyn added.

Taking only a sip each, they put the glasses down for later.

"I'll go first," Carolyn said. "It's shorter."

She explained how she and Mr. Cooper were re-called to London as a result of the attempt on Mrs. Thatcher's life, as had been the case for many operatives from across the world. As guilty as she had felt about leaving Bulgaria without seeing him, she had no choice. After a couple of days of exhaustive, and in her mind, wasted medical tests, she was re-assigned to Paris. She leaned forward to make a point.

"I had asked my mother to get the letter back, but as it turned out you had already opened it." She pulled a face. "You didn't get back to me, I knew you were in Ottawa for a couple of days, so Bob's your uncle; good bye Mr. Crowe."

They ordered their food from a most attentive waiter.

Ed outlined what had happened to him at the police station and the 'secret information' he had passed on the Bulgarian authorities. Carolyn burst out laughing when he explained the final piece of information he had provided.

"You called my father a tight-ass? That is funny. That is very funny."

"I had to make it clear that I knew what was going on, at least when the answers got back to London." Ed continued the story, leaving out any details of his stopover in Ottawa. "So two days ago, I got the letter you sent me and this time I read it in full."

"From my mother?"

He shrugged innocence. "It was special delivery."

She looked at him sideways. "Why would my mother send it on to you, Ed?"

"You're asking *me* to explain your mother to *you*?"

"There's something fishy here," she said, chewing on her bottom lip.

"May I continue?"

She waved him on.

"So I took the chance and flew here to see you." He smiled. "And here we are spending a quiet weekend in Paris. Just the two of us."

"There's more to this than meets they eye," Carolyn mused, now taking a sip of her wine.

"Maybe Mr. Cooper's correct. You have to trust the process."

"You trust the process, Mr. Crowe, I'll trust my intuition." She motioned to his drink. "Enjoy your wine, Ed, the business part is over. Let's just relax and enjoy our new-found friendship."

"Where to?" Ed asked as he hailed down a taxi.

"My place is best," Carolyn said, as the taxi pulled tot the curb. "I'm always on call. Beside I'd like you to see my flat. Nothing compared to Ankara mind you."

Six steps led up to the building where Carolyn lived.

"What is that?" Ed asked as the entered the lobby area.

"It's a lift. What does it look like?"

They stepped inside the lift. "Well I'd say it looks more like a dumb waiter to me. There's barely room for two people in here."

"It's the French style to keep people close," she grinned as she pressed the button for the eighth floor. "You know, love and all that?"

"Whatever you say, but it's about a quarter of the size of my apartment elevator."

"Oh, you North Americans—always worried about the size of things!"

"No comment."

"This way," she said, leading him down the hallway to her flat.

"This is nice," he said, looking around. "Hey, this is very nice. And look," he said, walking to the window, "you can see the Eiffel Tower."

"I'm glad you like it. It's your home, our home, for the next couple of days. There's a bottle of Champagne in the fridge. Why don't you open it and let's celebrate our renewed friendship?"

"Your wish is my command, madam," he offered walking to the fridge. "Anything for the lady I love."

She shook her head and smiled. If only, she thought.

CHAPTER NINETEEN

SATURDAY, OCTOBER 27TH

• • • • • • •

Ed woke with Carolyn snuggled in his arms. She was fast asleep and he moved slowly without waking her. He walked to the window, keeping back a few feet. He did not want to have her neighbors see him any more than they had to. It looked to be a fine day ahead, and they had planned a very touristy day of activity. He walked back to the bed and kissed her lightly on the lips.

"Good morning, sunshine. Time to wake up and cook food."

She opened one eye, smiled, and covered her head with the bed sheets. "I'm not an early morning person," she said through the linen. "Put the coffee on please. Nice and strong."

The phone by her side of the bed rang, and she sat up like a shot. It rang twice and then stopped.

"Probably wrong number," Ed called from the kitchen, searching for the coffee.

The phone rang again, and she let it ring. He stuck his head back into the bedroom wondering what was up. After the seventh ring it stopped. She held up her hand to warn him to not speak. The phone rang again and she picked it up before the first ring had ceased.

"Clear for go," she said quickly. She looked over to him and waved him out of the room.

He quietly and quickly left and went back to the kitchen. He could not hear her speak, but even so he hummed out loud to ensure he heard nothing. He made the coffee—she was still in the bedroom. He continued humming loudly, keeping his back to her bedroom.

"What are you doing?" she asked, standing at the bedroom door.

"Me? I'm just humming the Tchaikovsky Piano concerto number 1 in B-flat minor. Didn't you recognize it?"

"Actually I did. Is the coffee ready? We need to talk."

He poured two coffees and brought them to the table. She joined him, wrapping her housecoat around herself.

"Do you want me to leave?" he asked.

"I don't know. I'm thinking."

She drank her coffee, holding the cup with both hands. Her eyes were closed, deep in thought.

He drank his coffee trying not to make a sound, even as he sipped.

"Look, Ed," Carolyn finally said, "I have a job to do today, and guess what?"

"It doesn't include me."

"Wrong. It does include you—if you're interested that is. And I know you're interested. Only it has to be on my terms. I cannot express that enough, I . . ."

"Absolutely and completely understood," Ed interrupted.

"Okay, let me put some music on, just in case, and I'll top-up our coffee. I have an outline of a plan in my head."

Carolyn outlined the details of the phone conversation she had received from London, and her thoughts on how to accomplish the desired goals. "It's all a little short on time, since we only have four and a half hours to put it into action. What do you think?"

"I think it's very clever. I think the chance of success is good. And I think the down side risk is limited, but very real nevertheless."

'I hope you're not . . . ?" Carolyn started to say, but was interrupted.

"And I am not just saying this to go along with your idea. What I just said is exactly how I feel."

'Okay," Carolyn said, standing. "Let's get cleaned up and moving. Any equipment we need I have. All we need now is a bit of luck."

Ed didn't like the idea of wearing the same clothes he had worn the day before, but there was no choice. He was ready to go in half an hour. Carolyn was getting dressed in her bedroom. When she emerged from her bedroom, she stood at the door.

"How do I look?" she asked sheepishly.

"Holy Christ," Ed answered. "Do you ever look sexy."

"That's the goal I suppose." She gave a goofy look. "It's one of our official disguises, although I never thought I'd be wearing it."

She was wearing a French Maid's outfit, which superbly showed off her slim figure. The dress was mid thigh, and the dark stockings extenuated her long legs.

"I'm telling you, Carolyn, you look the role perfectly."

She looked at him with a frown. "Am I to be complimented that I look like a French whore?"

"In this case, I'm afraid so." He grinned, enjoying the view.

She lifted a small purse to chest height and opening it, bent to search for something in it. "Did you see anything?"

His eyes were wide open. "A nice amount of cleavage."

She shook her head. "I didn't mean that you toad. Did you see anything about my hat?" She leant over again.

"Not a thing, Carolyn. But let me make the point again. When you bend like that, a guy's not going to be looking at your hat. I'm sorry, but that's a fact."

"Okay, I take your point," Carolyn said, straightening the outfit. "God if my mother saw me in this she'd have a fit."

"You don't want me to take a photo then? You know, for the official records?"

"Don't be smart." She looked at the time. "Let's go over the details again."

They sat at the table and Carolyn went through the plan for the final time, step by step. They agreed it was workable.

"You're okay not wearing a gun?" she asked.

"Quite happy actually."

"Any other questions?" Carolyn asked.

He closed his eyes to think. "You're still going to make supper tonight? A special meal?"

She laughed. "Yes I am, and thanks for the vote of confidence!" She stood, leaned over and kissed him gently on his forehead. "Let's go, the car will be downstairs in five minutes."

At twelve-fifteen the limousine stopped in front of The Royal Monceau in the northern part of Paris. Carolyn stepped out, asking the driver, in French, to return in three hours. She wore only the French Maid outfit and carried the small purse with her. She stepped inside the hotel, keeping her head up. At the desk she enquired about her key. The gentleman checked his reservation book and handed her the key to room 422. She slipped it in her purse and walked up the four floors. There was no lift. When she arrived at the fourth floor, she took a deep breath and walked directly to room 424.

Standing in front of room 424, she took the room key out of her purse and tried the key. It did not work. She tried again, swearing in French as she did. She heard words from behind the door, and suddenly the door opened wide.

"What the fucking hell do you want?" the man asked. He was over six feet tall, with a strong Irish accent.

"Pardon?" she asked in French, stepping back in surprise.

"Who are you?" he asked, obviously annoyed, gesturing the other people in the room for silence.

"Mon chamber," Carolyn said, pointing into the room. "My room no?"

"It's newt your forking chamber," he said sarcastically with a French accent.

She held up the key. "Mon room usual!" she said.

He looked at the key. "You're next door for Jesus sake," he said, pointing the way.

She shrugged. "Okay, okay. Merci." She raised her purse and bent down to reach inside. She brought out a business card and handed it to him, smiling as sexily as she could. "Big man, no? When you in town, you call, yes?"

He took the card, shaking his head. "Me bloody old lady would kill me," he grinned. "But who knows—next time?"

He turned and closed the door. She could hear him laughing and joking to the other men in the room. She had seen three others. Two wore robes, and if she heard correctly, what little they said was in Arabic. She went into room 422. She quickly took off her hat, extracted the mini-camera, and put it in her purse. She took a miniature microphone out of her purse, walked to the window closest to room 424, and slipped off her shoes. She looked at her watch, and waited.

Six minutes later Ed walked along the corridor, rapped gently on the door to 422, and walked on to room 424.

"Bon jour," he said in English, knocking gently on the door.

"Now what the fuck?" the man said. Two seconds later the door swung open. The three other men had moved closer to the door, wanting to see what was happening.

"Hey it's mister fucking Romeo," the man said, stepping aside for the other men to see.

Ed stepped back in surprise, and spoke in his best American accent. "Who the hell are you guys? My girlfriend's rented this room."

"Girlfriend," the man laughed aloud, "some fucking girlfriend she is!" Then he laughed louder. "Or maybe she is."

"Hey, watch your tone buddy," Ed said. "No need to be crude."

"Mary, mother of God," the man exclaimed. "The Yank's got a mouth as large as his country." He leaned into Ed. "Your girlfriend, Mr. America, is in the next fucking room. Now get going, and don't make too much noise!"

The door slammed in Ed's face, and he could hear the laughter from inside the room. Ed walked to room 422 and knocked. Carolyn let him in.

"You gave me the wrong room number," he said aloud, but not shouting. Carolyn wasn't listening to him. She sat at a table. In the middle of the table was the smallest tape recorder Ed had ever seen. It was no more than four inches by two inches. It was running. She had an earplug attachment from the recorder to her left ear. Carolyn motioned for him to sit down, holding her fingers against her lips. He sat.

Next to the tape recorder were several sheets of hotel letterhead and a pen. He wrote, 'Working?' She nodded, with a smile.

They sat for over an hour, not speaking or writing. She adjusted the recorder from time to time, holding the earpiece in place. Suddenly she took the earpiece out, pointed to the bed, and put the recorder on the floor under the curtain. She jumped on the bed, rearranging it quickly. The bed was against the wall to room 424.

"Magnifique," she said in French. "Vous Americanos ouis!"

He scrambled for words. "You know how to make a man feel real good, my cheri."

They both moaned and groaned as if they were kissing.

"You so good," she purred. "Hmm, so good."

They heard banging on the wall from room 424 and a volley of laughter. They looked at each other, both rolling their eyes. She held her finger against her lips. She picked up the earpiece. "They're leaving," she whispered. They relaxed.

The knock on the door had them staring at each other in fear.

"One minute," Ed called out, taking off his clothes as quickly as he could. Carolyn jumped into the bed, covering herself up to her neck.

Ed stood by the door, wearing only his underwear. He opened the door slightly. The large Irishman was standing there, grinning.

"Gee, I thought you were the goddamned police," Ed said grinning, and opening the door a little wider.

"Or the lady's father maybe?" The man laughed. "Here, this is for you and your lady friend." He handed Ed a bottle. "Best Irish whiskey you can buy."

"Hey, thanks," Ed said. "I owe you one."

"Just say thanks to our friends in Boston," he winked.

"Sure, sure, okay. But I live in Minneapolis."

"Private joke," the man laughed. He turned and left.

"Thanks again," Ed called after him.

Ed had taken the bottle by the bottom. He carried it carefully to the table, and being careful not to touch it too much, he put it on the table.

Carolyn got out of bed and walked to the bathroom. "I desperately need a coffee," she said, "but first I need a pee."

Ed dressed and put the coffee maker on.

Sitting at the table, they drank warm but comforting coffee.

"That was close," she said.

"Closer than you think maybe."

"How's that?"

"If I'd been 'packing' as the Americans say, I'd have never got my pants off in time."

She laughed merrily. "Wouldn't that have been something? You standing there with a pair of trousers stuck on the bottom of your left leg. I'd have burst out laughing for sure."

"Well done, Carolyn," he said. "I think you're plan worked perfectly."

"Let's hope so," she said standing. "I have to get my stick-on microphone from the window and we can leave. Your conversation at the door gave me plenty of time, but it was sure scary." She walked to the window and turned to Ed. "Actually can you get it? I'm afraid of heights."

Ed walked to the window, opened it, and looked out. "How the heck did you get that on their window? I'm not afraid of heights but bloody hell."

He carefully climbed out and standing on the windowsill leaned across and unstuck the microphone. Just as carefully he climbed back inside.

"I know," she said, somewhat embarrassed. "That's why I needed to use the bathroom. I thought I was going to pee myself."

"Been there, done that," he said.

Carolyn took the limousine to the British Embassy, directing the driver to go via The Eiffel Tower and the Louvre and a ladies clothing shop. She wanted to ensure she was not followed. Ed went by taxi, changing taxis three times.

An hour later they stood in front of Terri at the Embassy reception desk.

"Nice coat, Miss Andrews. Cold out is it?"

"Is the ambassador ready to see us?" Carolyn asked.

Terri ignored the question. She turned to Ed. "Hello Mr. Dove. How are you doing today?"

"Just cooee thank you Terri. Free as a bird, so to speak."

The phone rang. Terri picked it up with a smile. "He'll see you now, Miss Andrews. Who should I say you're bringing with you?"

"An American from Minneapolis will be fine," Carolyn replied, walking toward the ambassador's office.

Ed followed her, waving back to Terri.

Carolyn knocked on the ambassador's door, and entered. Ed followed her in. The office was large with a boardroom table to the left. To the right were the ambassador's desk and four chairs facing it. The ambassador was younger than Ed expected. He stood as they entered and walked around the desk.

"Mr. Ambassador, I'd like you to meet Mr. Edwin Crowe. Mr. Crowe is a special operative working out of Canada. He works closely with the General." She turned to Ed. "Mr. Crowe, this is our ambassador in Paris, Sir Peter Edington."

They shook hands. The ambassador motioned them to be seated.

"Nice to have reinforcements, Mr. Crowe. Where are you from in Canada?"

"Oakville, Ontario, sir," he answered, "via Kensal Rise in London."

"Ah, Kensal Rise," the ambassador said. "Just northwest of Paddington station?"

"Yes, sir."

"Perhaps we can chat later. For now Miss Andrews, why don't you tell me how your day went?"

Carolyn explained in great detail the day's events, but leaving the impression Ed had only stripped to the waist when he answered the door. "The cameras from the hat and purse are in the lab sir, as is the bottle of whiskey."

"I am very impressed, Miss Andrews. I will have the film and tape converted and sent to London as a priority of course."

"Thank you, sir," she said. "I realize I took a chance using Mr. Crowe, but I couldn't think of how to accomplish the goal on such short notice without him."

"Taking a chance and making a decision are two different things, Miss Andrews. My report will reflect your making a decision."

Carolyn nodded. "Thank you. I appreciate that."

The ambassador ran his hand through his hair. "You realize, of course, that your . . ." Carolyn interrupted.

"Yes, sir. My written report will be complete."

"Then I suggest we leave things until Monday morning," the ambassador said, standing. "When do you leave Paris Mr. Crowe?"

"Late Monday, sir."

"Excellent," the ambassador said. "Then let us three meet Monday at, say, nine a.m., and see what you have captured."

He shook hands with both of them and walked them to the door.

"And, Miss Andrews. Keep the coat, but be sure to expense it. And that's an order."

"Yes, sir."

Ed and Carolyn walked to the front door of the embassy, under the watchful eye of Terri.

"Have a nice evening," Terri called to them.

They both raised their hands in thanks.

On the street, Ed started looking for a taxi.

"My first real action!" Carolyn said, gently punching the air.

"One question?" Ed asked.

"Proceed, my good sir," she replied, happy and proud.

"Will your report include the pee thing? Mine did." He hailed a taxi.

She gave him a dirty look, and got in the taxi.

Carolyn kept her coat wrapped around her until they were back in her apartment.

"Plus I get a new coat in the process," she said hanging it up.

"You do look a cracker in that outfit," Ed said, admiring the shortness of the dress. "Can I kiss you while you're wearing it?"

"I'm not sure that would be a good idea," she replied.

"In fact I'd like to make love to you while you're wearing it."

She pulled a face. "Don't talk dirty. It doesn't suit you."

She walked into her bedroom and closed the door. Ed started a pot of tea. The bedroom door opened. She stood in the doorway, still in the costume.

"Okay, get in here!" she said.

"I'm not going to wear that outfit again with you around," Carolyn said, buttoning her blouse.

"I'm sorry," Ed grimaced. "You're not mad at me are you?"

"Of course I'm not mad at you. I enjoyed every minute; not that there were many minutes mind you."

"Next time I'll go slower, honest."

"Who needs a next time after that?" She smiled at him, for some reason enjoying his embarrassment.

"I've got to get some other clothes." He wanted to change the subject.

"Perhaps you could try this little outfit on?" she asked, picking up the French Maid's costume from different parts of the room.

"Oh God," he mumbled.

She stopped picking up and turned to him. "For crying out loud, Ed, give over will you. We've just had the best sex we've had, and you're apologizing." She paused. "The quickest too perhaps, but who's complaining."

"I'm not even sure the kettle's boiled yet," he laughed.

They tidied up the bedroom and closed the door as they left.

"So what's for supper?" Ed asked, watching Carolyn pour over the cookbook.

"My specialty, Coq au Vin," she replied, checking her ingredients against the recipe.

"Specialty eh? Ever cooked it before?"

"No, but I'm told it's easy. And if it turns out to be easy, then it's going to be my specialty."

"Let me know if I can help."

"We each have a job," she said. "Mine is the food."

"Mais oui, I am the wine guy."

"Thought you'd never ask," she said, looking up from the book.

Ed poured them both a glass of wine. He stood over her as she worked on the meal.

"What kind of onions are they?" he asked taking a sip of his wine.

"Pearl onions."

"What is that?" He pointed at a green leaf.

"Thyme leaves."

"And that?" He pointed again

Carolyn stopped working, and held up both hands. "Ed, stop it. I'm doing my best here and you're putting me off. Do me a favor will you?"

"Yes, dear," he smiled.

"And don't call me dear!"

"Yes, older lady."

She sighed, pointing to the door. "Go downstairs. Get a taxi. Go to your hotel. Shower and shave; especially shave. Check out of the hotel and get back here within ninety minutes."

"Are you trying to make a point, Carolyn?" he asked nicely.

"Go!"

He left the apartment, bowing as he walked backwards to the door.

He returned within ninety minutes with his luggage and a bouquet of flowers. He presented her with the flowers. "For my second favorite older lady," he said.

She smiled as she took them. "I hope the first is your mother."

"Of course," he said.

She put the flowers in a vase, set them on the table, turned and gave him a huge hug.

"Set the table please, Ed. Dinner will be served in fifteen minutes."

As he was setting the table, he stopped to make a point. "The flowers are, in part, to congratulate you on your ingenuity and planning today. It was a very successful operation. I know your father will be very proud, and I suspect your mother will be somewhat perturbed."

"Because I wore the French Maid outfit?"

"No, because it was your first real action and it was successful."

She took a sip of wine. "You're probably right on both points." She carried the Coq au Vin to the table and served.

"Definitely a great meal," Ed said, helping Carolyn clean up. "You mother would be proud of your cooking."

"You seem to understand my mother better than I do, Ed. However I'll take that as a compliment."

They walked to the window looking out on the Eiffel Tower, which was now lit up. It was a beautiful view of the Tower and Paris. Ed put his arm around Carolyn and moved in close to her.

"Do you want to talk about us?" she asked.

He rolled his head from side to side. "Probably not."

"Oh!" she said with surprise. "May I ask why not?"

"Probably because if I got your letter and read it again, the most striking comment is, and I paraphrase . . . '. . . we will not grow old together . . .'"

He felt her move away from him just slightly. She turned to face the view of Paris. He squeezed her closer, but she did not move with the squeeze.

"Does that bother you that much?" she asked. "I thought we had somehow agreed to that point of view."

He let her go, and turned to face her. "Indeed we had and I fully understand the issue. It's just that I'd rather we talk about it on, say, Monday as you drive me to the airport. For now I'd like our weekend in Paris to stand on its own."

She smiled and kissed him on his cheek. "You are a romantic. But that's a good point. Monday it is."

"So what are your plans for us tomorrow Carolyn. What does a young couple do in Paris on a Sunday in October?"

"We get up at six a.m . . . ."

"Eight a.m."

"Seven!"

"Seven-thirty, for sure?"

"We get up at seven-thirty," Carolyn continued, "start with a continental breakfast, and then I'll take you to all of the tourist traps so that you can say you've seen all of what Paris has to offer. And further I'm going to show you the Paris that was designed by Baron Haussmann, and why other city designers and engineers have copied his work that created the current Paris. Let's go to bed. I'll tell you more about what I have planned for tomorrow."

CHAPTER TWENTY

SUNDAY, OCTOBER 28TH

• • • • • • •

Carolyn woke him up with a cup of tea in her hand. She was fully dressed and ready to go. Ed shook his head to wake up and sat up.

"You're up early," he said, taking the cup of tea.

"I've been working on my report for tomorrow," she smiled, "and planning today's tour of Paris. Drink your tea, and let's get going."

"I love you when so you're demanding."

Carolyn smiled. "You love me whatever I do."

"That's true, but you shouldn't be so sure you know?"

She reached over and ruffled his hair. "That's our discussion for tomorrow on the way to the airport. C'mon, move your tush." She turned and left the bedroom.

Ed finished his tea, pulling a face. He was not looking forward to that discussion. He knew in his heart it would not lead to an ending that he wanted. He knew that and accepted the fact. But accepting it didn't make it any better; probably worse. He slipped out of bed, determined to enjoy their remaining time together.

They had a lovely continental breakfast at a café close to Carolyn's apartment, and then she took Ed on a whirlwind tour of Paris. They traveled by bus, taxi and the underground Metro—whatever was the quickest an easiest way to get to the next stop. The Eiffel Tower, two hours at The Louvre, the Arc de Triomphe; The Champs Elysees, passing the Petit Palais and the Grand Palais on the way. They wandered along the Left Bank, admiring the many artists' works of painting and drawings. Carolyn allowed them time to grab a sandwich and coffee in the beautiful gardens of the Tuileries, and then they made their way to Notre Dame. They were now exhausted and took advantage of sitting in the stillness of the cathedral.

"So what do you think?" Carolyn asked, grinning at Ed as he caught his breath.

"You certainly know your Paris," he replied. "I'll have to visit again to remember anything in detail."

She smiled. "You know you're always welcome to visit me, if that was fishing for an invite."

"It was, and I'll keep the open invitation in mind. Speaking of which," he continued, "do you know how long you'll be here in Paris?"

She shook her head. "I never really know from day to day, but I'd suspect it will be a while. In spite of yesterday's activities, there is not a lot of undercover work in Paris, but that is more than compensated for by the social and networking opportunities available. Networking is big in my current world of work." She stood up, taking his hand to lead him on. "Let's go. I want you to learn all about how and why Paris was designed by Baron Haussman." He gladly followed, squeezing her hand gently as they left the cathedral.

Four hours later they were back in Carolyn's apartment, with a large map of Paris spread before them on the kitchen table.

"So you can see on the map, how all of Baron Haussman's work has left Paris a wonderfully designed city in which to live and visit." Carolyn was pointing out where they had visited since leaving Notre Dame. "You can see how by tearing down the old slums of the city and building the new avenues and boulevards it helped in better housing, better flow of traffic, and the new hospitals allowed for better medical care. In part it was designed to allow Napoleon's soldiers to move more quickly through the city, but this was not communicated as a goal. Which is not to say it was without controversy. Thousands of people were simply moved unceremoniously to the outskirts of the city, resulting in their land being taken over by the rich and famous." She shrugged. "But no one was going to challenge Napoleon who had commissioned the work. One of the largest and most famous additions was the Grand Opera House, designed, of course, by Charles Garnier."

"Of course," Ed agreed, "everyone knows that good old Charles designed the Paris Opera House." He grinned cheekily at Carolyn.

She started to fold the map. "Sorry, I suppose I am a bit boring carrying on about all of this. It's just so interesting to me."

He took her hand and kissed it. "It is interesting Carolyn, honest. But it has been a long day. I just want to kiss you for such a wonderful day, and then perhaps we could start on supper?"

She smiled, sat on his lap and kissed him gently. "You're an okay bloke, Ed. Now I'll start cooking, if you'd be good enough to select the wine."

She went to stand, but he pulled her back onto his lap. He kissed her neck and moved slowly up to her ear, kissing her as he did. "Just want you to know I love you—a great deal."

She kissed his forehead. "And I do you, Ed. Although I know I don't say it very often." They held each other tightly, and then stood to start working on their meal.

"And it's dinner, not supper," Carolyn said. "We're not in Canada now!"

Carolyn was working on the rack of lamb dinner while Ed was watching quietly, enjoying the red wine he had selected, when the phone rang. They both looked at it, expecting it to ring twice and then again a few moments later. It didn't. It kept ringing. Carolyn raised her eyebrows questioningly and picked up.

"Why, Mother, how nice to hear from you," Carolyn said, smiling at Ed. "What a pleasant surprise."

She listened for a moment.

"Actually I have a guest for dinner tonight. I'm working on a rack of lamb. I'd ask for your help, but . . ." She didn't need to finish the statement. Lady Stonebridge hadn't cooked for decades.

Carolyn looked surprised. "Why yes it is, Ed Crowe, Mother. How did you ever know?"

"Ah, yes of course, Father is aware of his being here."

"Yes he popped over to Paris and after our bit of business, I took the opportunity to invite him over tonight. He leaves for Canada tomorrow."

"No, Mother, there was no danger involved."

"No, Mother, I wasn't hurt. I am doing just fine, and have put the kidnapping behind me."

"Of course. I'll put him on." She held out the phone for Ed to take. He grinned, unsure of where this would head.

"Good evening Lady Stonebridge," he said. "It has been a while since we chatted."

"Good evening, Edwin," Lady Stonebridge said pleasantly. "I trust your meeting with my daughter has gone well."

"I am absolutely in love with Paris, Lady Stonebridge. It is now my favourite city."

"Very good. Very good. And how is my daughter taking it all?"

"Paris is wonderful. In full bloom, so to speak. Carolyn took me on a tour today, it was truly wonderful."

"Excellent, Edwin. Now don't let her get swayed too far. She needs a balance in her life. I don't know any of the details, but Lord Stonebridge is ecstatic about the results of your business dealings yesterday and he won't be afraid to let that be known to my daughter. The apple didn't fall too far from the tree, it appears! Remember that she thinks a great deal of you, Edwin. Please tell my daughter I'll phone her again on Tuesday."

"I think you're right, Lady Stonebridge. I'll pass on your message." He hung up the phone.

Carolyn closed one eye, and tilted her head. "You think my mother is right about what, and what message will you convey?"

"Your mother thinks Paris is a perfect location for you to be working in, I agreed, and she'll phone you Tuesday evening." He paused. "Presumably to check up on my trip to Paris!"

"I'm not sure about all of this, young man. There's something going on when my mother spends more time on the phone with you than with me."

He topped up their wine. "Don't be so suspicious for God's sake. She's your mother. I suppose she's just checking up on me."

Carolyn shook her head pondering his response, and went back to working on the lamb chops. Ed walked over to her and kissed her on the cheek. "Trust me, Carolyn. Remember I love you."

She pecked him back and waved him off with her greasy hands. "I have work to do. Why don't you put on some music?"

The lamb was beautifully cooked to medium and the potatoes were almost cooked. She grinned, as she tasted the potatoes. "Did it again, didn't I?" she asked. "Cooking is all in the timing it seems. Don't worry, next time I cook you a meal, the spuds will be over-cooked."

Ed put his knife and fork on his empty plate. "It was wonderful, Carolyn. Best meal you've ever cooked for me."

"It's only the third meal Ed."

"Still the best, Carolyn! I'm looking forward to the next meal and hope it won't be too long from now, you being an international traveler and all."

"Hmm, methinks you are into flattery young man."

Ed started cleaning the table. "I'll wash, you dry," he said. "Then I want us to put on some nice music, sit down, and hold hands."

They sat and talked for hours about themselves, being careful not to discuss any personal relationships in their respective pasts. At ten thirty Carolyn stood up and walked toward the bedroom. "It's been a long day, Ed, and tomorrow is an important day. I'm going to change for bed." She closed the bedroom door. Ed put their wine glasses in the sink and turned off the music.

The bedroom door opened and Carolyn stood in her French maid outfit, with a coy look on her face.

"Oh, my God," Ed said, walking toward her, unbuttoning his shirt.

"Now take your time, young man," Carolyn said, shyly covering her knees with her hands.

He reached her and took her in his arms. He kissed her neck and then asked quietly. "Can I fuck you, Carolyn?"

She looked up and smiled. "That would be lovely, Ed." She reached down, felt his erection, and lowered his zipper. "That would be very, very lovely."

CHAPTER TWENTY-ONE

MONDAY, OCTOBER 29TH 1984

••••••••

They were up early, had showered and cleaned up and Ed was packed
and ready to leave for Canada.

"That was pretty wonderful," Carolyn said smiling, tilting her head
to her bedroom and drinking the last of her tea.

Ed smiled back. "It was wasn't it? I love touching your body Carolyn,
especially when you enjoy it so much."

Carolyn blushed. "I'll miss you, Ed, and I love you very much."
She stood to leave. "Now let's get moving and get to the embassy
early."

In the Taxi ride to the embassy they held hands, sitting apart from
each other. Neither spoke: their weekend is Paris was over. Ed squeezed
her hand gently as the taxi pulled up in front of the embassy.

Terri was sitting at her desk when they entered. She smiled sweetly
as they walked across the large reception area together.

"Good morning, Miss Andrews, and good morning, Mr. Dove. How
are you both this lovely morning?"

"I'm sure we're both just fine Terri," Carolyn answered with a smile.
"And it's Mr. Crowe, remember?"

"My mistake," Terri said. She turned to Ed. "I understand you're a
bird watcher, Mr. Crowe. Do you prefer the birds here in France or those
in England, Mr. Crowe?"

Carolyn tried to interrupt the conversation, but Ed replied quickly.

"I prefer the birds that reside in both countries, Terri. They have a more international personality to them. They tend to be livelier, happier; perhaps because of the travel involved in daily lives?"

Terri nodded and winked at Carolyn. "Isn't that nice, Miss Andrews? I've never thought of birds in such a charming way. Mr. Crowe has such a nice way of expressing himself, doesn't he?"

"Yes it is and yes he does, Terri," Carolyn agreed. "Now is the ambassador ready to see us?"

"He asked me to send you right in. I'll arrange for tea. Have you both had breakfast?" She looked at them one at a time, smiling sweetly again.

"I have, thank you," Carolyn relied, turning to Ed for his response.

"So have I," Ed added.

Terri looked at Ed's bag. "You can leave your bag with me if you like, Mr. Crowe. I'll be sure to keep it close to me at all times."

"As you can see, Mr. Crowe," Carolyn said with a smile, "Terri has many talents. She not only looks after our guests, she handles all of our travel and expenses, she manages our fleet of cars, and some might say she is also the embassy gossip."

Terri smiled back. "I prefer to think of my role as an Information Dissemination Engineer. We are in the information age, are we not?"

Ed nodded, not wanting to get into the discussion. He thanked her and put his bag by her desk. She slid it under her desk with her foot. Ed and Carolyn walked toward the Ambassador's office.

"Cheeky devil," Carolyn commented.

"Cute though," Ed laughed. "Nice legs too."

Carolyn walked faster. Ed ran to catch up.

Ambassador Edington stood and welcomed them into his office with generous handshakes. He offered them to sit at the large table away from his desk and joined them.

"I am glad you arrived early," the ambassador said. "Lord Stonebridge will be phoning at nine-thirty, and as you know, Miss Andrews," he said looking at her, "he is always prompt."

"Always, sir," Carolyn said.

"Tell me this first, Miss Andrews. How much of the conversation you recorded did you actually hear and understand?"

She thought for a moment. "Not a lot really. They were whispering for most of the conversation, and I hoped the taping picked up more than I did. The only time I completely understood was when they spoke about listening in to the activity in the room we were in." She chose her words carefully.

Ambassador Edington nodded. "As we suspected. Yes the recording was excellent and, I might add, extremely informative." He paused to make his point. Both Carolyn and Ed sat up in their seats, now curious to hear what news was forthcoming. Ed remembered that Lady Stonebridge had indicated about Lord Stonebridge's being 'ecstatic' as a result of Carolyn's plan. He looked sideways at Carolyn, but her eyes remained fixed on the ambassador.

The ambassador took a deep breath and began his summary. "When you were contacted Saturday morning, Miss Andrews, all we knew was that members of the Libyan army were to meet at the hotel with a terrorist organization to discuss the sale of Semtex. Semtex, before you ask, is a plastic explosive that has been manufactured in Libya for years, and sold to anyone that has the money. We were aware of the meeting from a highly trusted contact in Libya. What we didn't know until we listened to the tape recording and exposed the photos that you took was that the other organization in the room was the IRA."

"Oh, my God," Carolyn gasped, covering her mouth. "I think I know where this is going."

The ambassador nodded. "I'm sure you do. The conversation makes it clear that it was Semtex previously purchased from Libya that was used in the Brighton Bombing earlier this month. And to add even greater clarity, it is clear from the conversation that the contact from the IRA in the room, a Patrick Magee, was the person that set the bomb at the hotel. The photos and the fingerprints from the whiskey bottle make it uncontroversial. We now know our man, and we're sure they are not aware of our findings."

Ed swallowed hard, taking in the facts. "Bloody Hell, Carolyn! Well done! This is amazing."

"Bloody Hell indeed, Miss Andrews," the ambassador said. "You've made us all proud" He paused. "Having said that, however, please bear in mind that this will be known to very few people, and only those with the highest level of security. In fact we are the only three people here in the embassy who know. Our congratulatory remarks must be limited and muted."

"Yes, of course. Thank you, sir," Carolyn said. "I confess I'm a little stuck for words. Amazing what a change of clothes and some bad acting will do."

Ed kept his eyes on the ambassador, not wanting to meet Carolyn's eyes as she referred to the French Maid outfit.

"Yes indeed," the ambassador agreed. "And well done, Mr. Crowe, for your part of the plan."

"Thank you, sir. But best-supporting role at most!"

There was a knock on the door, and a trolley of tea was rolled into the office. Terri smiled at them "Made it myself," she said. "Not often we get guests from Canada." She gave a brief curtsy and left the room.

"She's in a fine mood for a Monday morning," the ambassador said, getting up to pour the tea.

"I think she fancies Mr. Crowe," Carolyn said coyly, grinning at Ed as the ambassador's back was turned.

"Really?" the ambassador asked. "Well you could do a lot worse than our Terri. Her father is a Member of Parliament. Labour Party mind you, but not a bad sort." He began pouring the tea.

They each drank their tea watching the phone in the center of the table, waiting for it to ring. When it rang, at exactly nine-thirty, it still made them jump slightly. The ambassador answered the phone on speaker.

"Good morning, Lord Stonebridge," he answered, "the three of us are here. You are on speaker-phone sir, and the line is secure."

Lord Stonebridge's voice was clear and crisp. "Good morning, Mr. Ambassador, and good morning, Miss Andrews, and, Mr. Crowe. It is indeed a fine day."

Carolyn and Ed wished him a good morning, both unusually nervous. They knew it would be a positive conversation, but the implications of their actions were more important than they had anticipated.

"I have briefly explained the results of the tape recording and photos to our guests," the ambassador said. "Needless to say, they are both surprised and pleased with the results."

"And so you both should be pleased," Lord Stonebridge replied. "My congratulations to you both. A well thought out plan, Miss Andrews. Well done."

Carolyn leaned onto the phone. "Thank you, sir. I'm sure I would have been more cautious if I had known who we were listening in on."

"Don't limit your successful thought process and planning, Miss Andrews," Lord Stonebridge said. "It was a well thought out, clean, and simple operation, and put in place with very little time."

Carolyn blushed slightly. "Thank you."

"And, Mr. Crowe," Lord Stonebridge continued, "how opportunistic that you were in Paris at the time."

"Yes, sir. Just on a brief personal visit," Ed said. "My first time in Paris."

"We will have to change that, Mr. Crowe. Please submit your travel and hotel expenses to London. I am most reluctant to describe such a successful operation as happenstance."

"Yes, sir. Thank you, sir."

Lord Stonebridge continued. "I assume, Miss Andrews, you have a draft report written?"

"Yes, I do sir," Carolyn replied.

"Good," Lord Stonebridge said. "Now please read it aloud. I want to ensure it reflects as precisely as possible the facts as we now know them. Let us recall that five people died and more than thirty people were injured in the Brighton bombing. This is of great importance."

Carolyn took the report from her purse and started reading. Agreed-upon changes were made including adding the comments made to Ed about 'our friends in Boston'.

"I will have it re-written and on the ambassador's desk by nine a.m. tomorrow morning," Carolyn said, happy with the changes.

"Excellent work again, Miss Andrews," Lord Stonebridge said, "I will let you all get back to work, and thank you again for your time."

Ed leaned into the phone. "Please pass on my regards to Lady Stonebridge."

"I will do that," Lord Stonebridge answered.

"Mine too," Carolyn added with a smile.

"I will do that for sure, Miss Andrews," he laughed. "I will be sure to pass on your regards."

Ambassador Edington wrapped up the meeting, passing on his own thanks and congratulations. "I am very glad that I selected you, Miss Andrews, to head up this operation. It is not very often one gets mentioned in papers."

Ed shrugged his lack of understanding.

"What the ambassador is referring to," Carolyn explained, "is that his name would have been included in Lord Stonebridge's report to the PM as it relates to the success of the operation."

Ambassador Edington smiled. "And all I did was select the right person for the right job. Rest assured however that both of your names will be reflected in my report, a copy of which will be sent to CSIS in Ottawa, Mr. Crowe."

Ed smiled and thanked him, wondering if that was all good. He and Carolyn left his office, and headed back to the reception area.

Terri slid the bag from under her desk. "Will you be visiting us again, Mr. Crowe?" she asked, smiling at Ed.

"I don't think so," Ed replied, picking up his bag.

"Well if you do, you can always leave your bag with me, Mr. Crowe."

"That's very generous of you Terri," Carolyn said. "May we go now?"

"Of course, Miss Andrews," Terri smiled. "Which car would you like, Miss? The Jaguar or the Austin?"

"I'll take the Jag. Nice to be driving a solid English car in Paris."

Terri gave her the car keys and wished Ed 'Au revoir'.

Carolyn pulled the Jaguar out of the Embassy compound and was quickly doing forty miles an hour. After Ed gripped the dashboard and closed his eyes, she slowed down. She looked over at Ed and smiled. "Now about us," she said.

Ed shrugged. "Okay what about us? I love you. You love me. I'm a travel agent who lives in Oakville, Canada. You're a highflying civil servant with the British government who one day hopes to be an ambassador. Today you're in Paris, tomorrow—who knows where you'll be? My mother thinks the world of you and your mother thinks I'm an okay bloke. Oh! and I have a not-real Canadian passport and a part-time job working for the MI6! Pretty run-of-the-mill stuff, I'd say." He paused. "And by the way, this is the fourth time you've driven around the Arc de Triumph in the past two minutes."

Carolyn took a turn and headed down the Champs Elysees.

"I do have some news," Carolyn said, keeping her eyes on the road.

"Good or bad?"

"You tell me."

"Go ahead."

"Peter Reynolds's phoned me last week."

"Oh my."

"He asked me to marry him."

"Oh God!"

"I told him I'd get back to him this week."

"Oh shit."

"Please don't swear, Ed."

"Okay."

Carolyn pulled the Jaguar over to the side of the road, parked and turned off the engine.

"You can't park here," Ed said, pointing to the sign.

"Yes I can. The car has diplomatic plates."

"That's cheating."

"That's life."

"That's true." He shook his head. "I thought he was engaged to someone else."

"He is. He'd have to cancel it if—"

"Charming, I'm sure."

Carolyn turned to face him. "So?"

"So what?"

"So what do I tell him?"

Ed pulled a face. "For God's sake, Carolyn, you can't ask my opinion on that."

She smiled gently. "I can, and I am. If I hadn't met you a few months ago, I'd probably be arranging my wedding now—with great assistance and enthusiasm from my mother. My life would be looking a great deal different than it is now." She paused. "So?"

"So what did he say?"

"He told me that he loved me; always has. He wants us to get married, and raise a family on the parcel of land that his parents will give us as a wedding gift. Twenty acres. He thinks in a few years he will make enough to buy a small place in France for our annual get-away. He'll make partner next year."

"That's pretty good. Sounds like a lovely life."

"Yes, it does."

"Does your mother know he phoned?"

"Of course."

"What did she say?"

"Much to my surprise she said I have to make up my own mind, and wouldn't offer an opinion."

"That's unusual. Your mother has a point of view on most every thing."

"That's what I thought. I wondered if she thought I might do the opposite of what she thought."

"That's a lot of thought."

She leaned over and punched his arm. "Please, Ed, what do you think I should do?"

Ed rolled his eyes. "I think you should marry him."

"What?" she shouted. "You think I should marry him?"

"You're worrying the nice policeman just outside your window," Ed said, pointing.

Carolyn rolled down the window and spoke briefly to the police officer. He saluted and walked away.

Carolyn turned back to Ed. "I'm sorry. I didn't mean to shout."

Ed smiled. "I haven't seen you that mad before."

Carolyn shook her head, and spoke slowly. "Why do you think I should marry him, Ed?"

"Because it will lead to the best life available to you right now. You can continue your career, probably in London, and if you do get to be an ambassador, as I'm sure you will, it won't look too shabby to have the ambassador's husband being a well known Barrister from Smith, Smith, Smith, and Smith. He'll probably be a Q.C. by then. That all sounds pretty attractive, Carolyn."

"Yes, I suppose it does, but . . ."

"But," he interrupted, raising his hand, "I don't think for a minute you are going to say yes." He shook his head seriously. "Not in a million years are you going to say yes. But if you do," he continued, "I want you to know that I'll pull a Benjamin Braddock."

"A what?"

"Benjamin Braddock; played by Dustin Hoffman in *The Graduate*. I'll stand at the back of the church in Aylesbury, and scream . . ."

"In Little Kimble," Carolyn interrupted solemnly. "We planned on getting married in the church in Little Kimble. Just down the road from Stonebridge Manor."

"You planned this last week?" Ed gagged.

"When we were ten," Carolyn groaned. "We planned it when we were ten for God's sake." She wiped her eyes quickly. "What a brat I turned out to be."

Ed pulled on his ear, not sure what to say. "Look I'm sorry. I wasn't trying to make fun of the situation. But I don't think you're going to say yes, Carolyn."

She looked at him, her eyes slightly puffed. "Why are you so sure, Ed?"

"Because, Carolyn, you don't love him, and I doubt he loves you. If he truly loved you he would have flown to Paris, got down on his knees, and begged you to marry him. Heck I flew to Paris, and I'm sure not going to ask you to marry me."

She wiped her eyes. "And why not, might I ask?"

"Because, Carolyn, you'll say no. Or more to the point, you won't say yes. I'd rather not ask than be told no. How does the saying go? It's better to remain silent and thought a fool, than to speak up and remove all doubt."

"I'm not going to comment on that," she said, now smiling.

"I do have a proposal for you though, Carolyn. If you want to hear it that is?"

"Of course I want to hear it."

"Is there a pub in Little Kimble?" Ed asked.

"Yes, The Swan Inn. It's actually half way between Little Kimble and Great Kimble."

Ed thought for a moment. "Well, in exactly one-thousand-eight-hundred-and twenty-four days, I will get on my knees at The Swan Inn in Little Kimble and ask you to marry me."

Carolyn looked at him in amazement, repeating the number.

"That's five years, 1988 is a leap year. So October 29th 1989, I'll be at the pub looking for you. I'm guessing in five years you will be in a position, both personally and in your career, to at least consider my proposal of marriage. I know it's an arbitrary date, Carolyn, but we'll both be thirty-two, and perhaps ready to settle down?" He shrugged.

"I'm not sure what to say to that, Ed."

"Please don't say anything. Let's not mention it again between now and then. Let's continue our friendship as it is. You phone me and I'll join you wherever you are in the world. Or you can visit me anytime you like."

"Are you sure you're okay with that? It's asking a lot of you."

"I'm fine with it, Carolyn. On the assumption you're not going to say 'yes' this week that is."

"Oh, I suppose I knew I would say 'no' to Paul. If I had any inclination to think positively about his question, the results of our operation this weekend eliminated that. I'm planning on submitting a request to officially join the Brighton Bombing assignment. I've seen the man, and I don't like him." She turned to Ed. "So you see my work is too important to give up for a future second-home in France, etc. It just all seems a little unfair. I don't want to hurt his feelings, and I do want you to continue loving me. It's all very selfish of me."

"No matter, Carolyn. Like the other man said in the other movie . . . 'We'll always have Paris'."

"Shut up, Ed," Carolyn said, turning forward and starting the engine. "You'll have me in tears, and I don't like crying women."

"Yes, dear."

"And don't call me dear."

"Yes Miss Andrews."

She turned and smiled at him. "I love it when you call me Miss Andrews."

CHAPTER TWENTY-TWO

FRIDAY, NOVEMBER 2ND 1984

• • • • • • •

Many of the customers of the Queen's Head were in Halloween costumes. A tough-looking Margaret Thatcher mask was popular with the ladies. It was Ed's first taste of Halloween and he enjoyed the humor it offered at the time of year when the days were getting shorter and the nights colder.

"No costume?" Karen asked as she pulled a pint of Double Diamond for him.

"I'll have one next year for sure," he replied.

Karen put his pint on the bar. "Missed you last Friday."

"I was in Paris," Ed said, tasting his beer.

"Must be nice. Business or pleasure?"

"Mostly business. Got the full one-day tour. First time for me."

"Are the taxi drivers still as friendly?" Karen laughed.

"Especially when they hear an English accent. It makes them even more superior than normal."

Karen nodded. "And that's saying something."

Karen served other customers and came back to Ed. "Where are the girlfriends you used to bring in? Young man like you shouldn't be drinking alone on a Friday night."

"I've always got you to talk to," he smiled.

"You and another twenty customers, but thanks for the thought."

Ed took another sip of beer. "Actually they're both living in different cities. It's all so global nowadays."

Karen nodded as she pulled a pint for another customer. "That's true. My parents are always telling me how a trip to the Isle of Wight from London was such a big trip. Now people fly across Europe for a cheap weekend visit."

Karen worked her way down the bar serving the increasing number of visitors. Ed finished his beer and waved goodnight.

"Just one beer tonight?" Karen asked.

"You've got me thinking," Ed replied, pulling on his jacket.

Feeling both nervous and self-centered, he dialed Pat's number in Ottawa. It was ten thirty. Not too late he hoped. She answered it on the second ring.

"Hi, Pat, it's me—Ed."

"Really? I'd never have recognized your Canadian accent."

"Yeah good day, eh!"

"How are you, Ed?"

"Fine. Do you have a couple of minutes, Pat?"

"Sure, I'm just sitting here with my boyfriend."

Ed was caught off guard, and stumbled. "Oh! boyfriend, sorry I didn't . . . Look I'll phone another time."

Pat laughed. "Don't be silly, Ed. I'm sitting here with Robin."

"Ah, my favorite cat. That's good. I mean . . ."

"Ed you're mumbling." She paused. "How was Paris?"

He took a breath. "Fine. Just fine. Interesting weekend. I suppose you got a copy of the report?"

"I am your overseer in Canada, Ed. Not your boss. More like a handler."

"Look I . . ."

Pat interrupted. "Are you phoning to cancel our June trip, Ed?"

He took a deep breath and licked his lips. "No, Pat, no I'm not. Actually I was going to ask you if we could get together before June. I don't seem to be doing a very good job of asking however."

"Let me see," she said. Ed could hear a rustling of papers, which continued for what seemed forever. "Well, first there's November and that's pretty busy," Pat said, almost to herself. "Then there's Christmas and all that. How about the middle of January, Ed?"

"Oh!"

"Oh?"

He chewed his lower lip. "I was thinking of tomorrow."

"Tomorrow?" She paused. "As in Saturday tomorrow?"

"Yeah, sort of Saturday tomorrow." He shrugged. He listened, waiting for a reply. Unsure of what to say, he continued waiting. Pat came back on the line.

"I'll be at your place tomorrow at ten a.m. Have the tea on. We'll drink it on your balcony."

He smiled, and his voice showed it. "Thanks, Pat, you're a true friend. Can I pick you up?"

"I'll make my own way." She sounded happy. "I'll be there at ten."

"Terrific, that will give me time to clean the place up a bit. I'll make us a nice brunch, okay?"

"Listen, Ed," Pat spoke sincerely, "let me say this on the phone: it's easier for me. You mean a great deal to me, and I love you for phoning me today. I'll be at your door tomorrow morning at ten. Good night, Ed." She hung up before he could respond. He put the phone down quietly.

Ed quickly made a list of the things he had to get done by ten the next morning. He was excited about Pat's visit. He looked at the list again, and where he had written 'clean linen' he added 'both beds'. Then he added, 'pick up flowers'.

He got to bed early going over in his head the things he wanted to have ready for Pat's arrival.

When he fell asleep he was thinking and dreaming of Carolyn.